VISITING THE BARD

Alasdair Campbell

VISITING THE BARD

and other stories

First published in Great Britain in 2003 by Polygon
an imprint of Birlinn Ltd

West Newington House
10 Newington Road
Edinburgh

www.birlinn.co.uk

ISBN 1 904598 02 1

The publishers acknowledge subsidy from the Scottish Arts Council
toward the publication of this volume.

Scottish
Arts Council

British Library Cataloguing-in-Publication Data
A catalogue record for this book is available on request
from the British Library

Typeset by Palimpsest Book Production Limited,
Polmont, Stirlingshire

Printed and bound by Creative Print and Design, Ebbw Vale, Wales

for
CATHERINE
MAGGIE
IAIN
and
ELAINE

Contents

Things went well for him at first. Even his wife seemed to have settled down. But one day, he belted a girl for dumb insolence. That night, three men came to the back door of the schoolhouse. "You'll be leaving," they told him. In our district, he would have got off with it. But he happened to be in the district of Uig. Strange people live in Uig. I wouldn't like to be a blind man there.

The Oilman and the Uncles

Back on the island, on a loose scree clifftop at the back of Aird, flat grey skelfs of Lewisian gneiss shift, clattering, under your feet, as your rig boots seek then secure a purchase, the district of Ness extends to your right in a blue haze, a darker blue stripe of road running through it, and under a high flaring sky, the Atlantic, streaked with tidal rips and currents, stretches beyond the faint curving rim of the world, impossibly huge in the glistening space of afternoon light. Over the limitless waters, a deep-ocean wind sweeps cloudshadows, snaps the trousers against your braced legs, brings tears to your eyes. Confronted with this immensity, a primeval fear baits your breath, turns your stomach to ice – where is your defiance now? where is all your arrogance? On the Dell skerry, five cormorants take turns at hanging their wings to dry; heads mobile as weavers' shuttles move incessantly on long flexible necks to check the Toe of Galson in a mica glitter to the south, the long finger of the Butt of Lewis to the north. Mariners' mark, forever fixed, today the dull blue of Ballachulish slate; at her base, a restive sea heaves languidly, breaks in white spurts, subsides again. Out there, the unrecovered hundred and twenty-year-old bones of six men from this village await a promised resurrection; where sunlight dazzles and dims on Sannda bay, thirty-one Nessmen drowned one hysterical December day, claimed within sight of shore, their womenfolk watching from the leas. Mild windless morning it was they put to sea; fathers, sons, brothers, sweethearts, booted and gansied, shouldering skaals; a single small ignorable cloud on the horizon. The oxblood American redwings, so sure of their grip on the deck of an oilrig, commence another slow slide among the green and saffron-spotted stone platters; you alter your stance, tilt into the blow. White air races.

Isolated and unyielding townships, each hugging its own memorials of past agonies and cruelties. A segregated, seagoing people. Outlaws came here from the mainland, crooks and cheats, perpetrators of ancient insurance scams, all on the run, fleeing the wrath of their fellows. An Gobha Gorm, bearing a blue, barely healed gash down one side of his face, a going away present from the Sutherland Mackays. An Cleistear from Colonsay; a Campbell, a thief. Vikings, when black winds were combing the sea's hair white, found it treeless and flat as the lands to the north from which they'd fled. The dwarf people who set their puny scrawls and scars at the sea's edge before Eoropaidh was Eoropaidh, Sgigersta Sgigersta, Ness Ness, emerging from their underground dwellings one morning to sniff the air, take the first piss of the day, stop to goggle aghast at a galley beached in the rivermouth, stogged ten points off the perpendicular, sail hanging slack, dragonshead prow leering up at the slopes; one long northman with close-set eyes and an axe at his belt already ashore, scratching his bullybag, ruminating on possibilities. Progeny of both still here: beak-nosed, jug-eared blond giants, immaculately overalled, menders of punctures, groaners of graces over the brothplate; small dark gabblers, setters of mousetraps in bare cupboards, the earth on fire beneath their feet, high summer ragwort threatening to flytrap their balls. With all that comes between … An errant gust catches you side-on, triggers a brief, high-stepping raindance on the stones before spinning you round to face the land. Spread your arms wide as the breeze puffs out your anorak, slaps the hood smartly over the back of your head, balloons your trousers at the front into long sausage shapes. Miracleman on Ness clifftop prepares to fly, unaided by mechanical contrivance of any kind. In his dreams he can. Hovering above the cobwebbed lightshade, contemplates heads of Cratchit family round the kitchen board, swoops, nabs a potato from Tiny Tim's plate. Descend, still earthbound, digging in your heels, to a sward of dark-green grass, springy, like a lawn, flowing from where the scree peters out on the land side into the next grey outcrop strewn with loose debris. Sea pinks wave between the stones, cling to the rock ledges further down. Away from the cliff edge, boulders heave out of sloping ground amid patches of moss and sour-looking heather scrub. Whose sheep these are that raise their heads at your approach but do not run, you haven't the foggiest. Bedraggled blackfaces, one scrawny Border Leicester, marked with red across their haunches, hooped ribs showing through their unfed sides. Why aren't they on the moor? No sheep go out on the moor now, she rides in windy blue emptiness, her shielings tumbled, sheep trails vanished, streams and bogholes overgrown with moor grass and heather. The Galson river is choked at source. While back at the double-glazed, centrally-heated ranch, the crofter's fenced policies go down to the sea, rabbits run amok now the dogs can't get at them through the rylock and barbed wire, sheep batten on bad grass where corn and barley and potatoes and turnips once waved green and yellow all summer long, charged the autumn air with a perfume that weighted your heart. Are you walking to the Broad Shore? Long way to go in these bloody boots. A cross-eyed scavenger from England is sometimes to be encountered in the geos hereabouts, rubber-gloved and oilskinned, rootling among bladderwrack and oarweeds, but not today. Today, only the ghosts of the dead accompany you on your slipping and sliding progress. You knew them, the men whose places these were, recall their weatherbeaten faces, narrowed, horizon-scanning eyes, dungarees faded from washing and patched at the knees on the inside. Straightening from the spade, *oich oich*, hand outstretched: *You're back.* Invisible at the end of long bamboo rods, flyfishing for saithe from sheerly accessible rockshelves shining with sea damp. In the middle of the Dell fank, men bawling, dogs barking, sheep milling and baaing, raised stour settling on eyelashes, inside nostrils, your mother whispers severely of one of them: *His two hands murdered live people in the*

[3]

war in Crete. Long fellow in a bib overall, greasy tweed bonnet: William John's Angus. One of the two hands that murdered live people in Crete is carrying a live lamb by its forelegs. Now, as you teeter gracelessly down into Diobadail and cross the pebbled beach, strewn above the high water line with plastic floats, bottles, fishboxes, pallets of driftwood, a sheep's carcase picked to bleached bone on top, orange mottled skin crackling and singing in a grey silt stench beneath, they walk beside you, over the scars of peatbanks long unworked, the pale green hummocks of lazybeds long unturned, flitting quietly about you, the ghosts of men whose haunts these were, out of the old times, the old days. Cars of the living flash out on the main road, leave the telegraph poles standing. A world of contracts and commissions, of crouchbacked telephones and windowed manilla envelopes, goes about its business. Far from all these, above the Broad Shore, the wind suddenly changes direction, swerves away from you northwards, to Iceland, to nowhere; the flying air stilled as if mighty hands had twisted an invisible cowl in the sky. Here the sea breaks far out on the Galson side, slides into the bay around a high-tide skerry from which, on September nights so quiet you could hear dogs barking in the village two miles away, you fished for cuddies by the light of the moon. Terns nesting on the green-capped central rock will erupt in a white frenzy if you venture onto the shingle below, screech in to the attack from all angles – and how, lacking a protective plastic helmet, perspex goggles, shepherd's crook gripped at the straight end and whirled dementedly clockwise above your head, are you to ward them off? No, better stay where you are, in the sudden strange lull, let your visiting shadow slant over the graves of two unknowns who sleep here, side by side, at the crumbling sea's edge. They weren't big men, if men they were. Greyish-blue stones, one jagged, one squarish, like ancient sown stumps of teeth, mark their resting place. They are buried correctly, they will rise on the first morning of eternity to face the sun. In the continuing lull, a faint puff of wind lightly buffets your face. Precursor:

the wind chap. The dog before his master. Behind it, far out to the west, in the vaporous cradle of storms, a new sea, churned by the wind, is rising even now to come charging in on the land, sapphire and malachite towers, terrific in height, lit from within, thundering shorewards, their forked white crests, tipped with gold, flying backwards, the sea for a mile out scooped up before them, laying bare the thousand reefs of the Broad Shore to the chaotic sky, before the oncoming mass of waters, roaring and crashing, overwhelms them again. Fearful of the approaching hurricane, seabirds sail inland. You, too, before the wind. Before the great storm comes. Bunch your hands in your anorak breastpockets and set your face for the village. Your lies and follies, vain boastings and daylight blasphemies, do not signify here; your courage in the face of small danger, and boldness where there was little to fear, count for nothing.

2

Old Peter, oldest man in the village, uncle, grand-uncle, great grand-uncle, sits at the fireside in a high-backed tubular-steel chair with a thin white plastic seat and white plastic armrests. The chair is the property of the Social Services, Stornoway, and it is only in Peter's house on loan. Five women – a health visitor, a district nurse, two home helps and his late sister Willina's daughter Maggie, married in Plasterfield – conspired to get it for him. It possesses orthopaedic and therapeutic qualities beyond ordinary armchairs; telephones were lifted, forms filled in, a birth certificate found and photocopied, and following a visit from an assessor (woman number six, a large babbling brook) the chair arrived in the back of an ambulance, brand new, still in the polythene. Peter doesn't like it.

"I don't like it," he tells his nephew, the oilworker, back on the island from the North Sea.

"Yes, you do!" the evening home help yells from the kitchen.

"They make me sit in it."

"No, they don't!" the home help yells, above a torrential tap.

Aged eighty-five now, oldest man in the village, third oldest in the district and the last of the family. Summoned at 10 p.m. on a Monday night of the seven elements without, gasps and groans within – each gasp and groan echoed accurately from the other side of the wooden partition separating the bedroom from the fire by a spinster aunt, his mother's sister, who was otherwise no help at all – the midwife moved the tall paraffin lamp to the head of the bed at 5 a.m. on Tuesday morning and spoke as follows: "I am giving you not one boy child but two. This one" – handing his brother Donald to her – "is already a made child. But" – holding Peter to the light and sternly shaking her head – "it will be many a day before you make a man of this one."

Peter after a grand-uncle on the distaff, a poacher and nodder at lintels, who had been in the Shanghai police and died in Raigmore Hospital, Inverness, aged thirty-four; killed by chloroform while getting a gamekeeper's pellets removed from his leg. Donald was named after their father's uncle. From the trenches in France, their father approves Donald, suspects collusion in the case of Peter, says there is a lot of deaths about, says to tell his father if the ram comes back from the moor not to let him go again, to kill him. He gets leave, gets to Kyle of Lochalsh gets no further (typhus scare in the Outer Hebrides) returns to the trenches by way of Glasgow. Back in Kyle of Lochalsh after the Armistice, is one of the few not to have nearly boarded the *Iolaire*, and makes it over to Stornoway on the *Sheila*. He lifts Donald into the air. "Peter," he says. Thick black moustache, hard-knuckled man's hands selecting seed potatoes, baiting a tarred handline. He teaches them a song: "Mad mossel from Arminears, paalee voo." Peter remembers brightly polished black boots and a silver watch chain on Sundays . . .

"There!" The home help plants a tray on Peter's lap.

Scrambled eggs. Mug of tea. Bun with a dusting of sugar on top.

"Thia!" ruffling the nephew's hair with a red, soda-chapped hand, "how did it get so white? Do you take milk and sugar?"

. . . remembers in lowermost December, from a neighbour's window, through air heavy as water, a funeral passing: men in long gaberdine coats holding hats to their left ears against the wind. He sees his father inside the coffin: puts his head on the other twin's shoulder. Hears his father, inside the coffin, singing. Their older brother, also Donald, called Dan, comes away from the window, goes to a bedroom, lies on the bed, faces the wall, pulls the pink quilt over his head. The wardrobe door has a piece of *Daily Express* wedged in it to keep it shut. Their mother, strange in a black dress, black stockings, says, "Say your prayers. Till your aunty Crissie hears you." On the mat beside the bed, on their knees. Peter first: "Mercy on a small sinner for Christ's sake. Amen." Donald (ten minutes older): "Mercy on a big sinner for Christ's sake. Amen." Spoon fashion in the big double bed, fierce black night outside. Donald's arm round Peter, Peter butted against him. The wind whooms against the gable end, the sea booms at the back of Aird, the turned-down lamplight flickers inside its globe. Donald's arm tightens around Peter. Our Father who art in Heaven.

"Egg brose," he says, and prods the yellow conglomerate on his plate with a fork. "So what has she put on the bun this evening?" Blinks at the nephew, his filmy old man's eyes, a thin line of sticky white curd rimming both eyelids.

"Never you mind what she put inside the bun!" comes the high response from the kitchen.

(She can hear the grass growing.)

"Red rat poison!" she shouts.

"When did you come out of the North Sea?" he asks the nephew.

"Tuesday. Monday night."

"And where have you been staying?"

"Harris."

"Why don't you stay here anymore? Your room's still here."

"It's just . . . I've this friend in Harris . . ."

"I'll let you beat me at draughts. Eat that," he says, shoving the bun across. "Don't let on to her."

Motions to the nephew, *take the tray*, sits back in the miraculous, tubular-steel chair, round-bellied, stubby fingers twitching as though he were memorising a pipe tune on an invisible chanter. Plump red cheeks, snub nose with a fine network of veins at each nostril. Swollen, pipe-puffing lips. He looks like a retired cherub. Something whistles in his chest. Not looking at the nephew, he starts to mutter,

"Donald Kenneth, the Bard's brother, was on the *Hood*. I watched her sail out of Scapa Flow to engage the Bismarck. What did they know? What did we know? John Norman Handy was with me on the convoys," he continues, not pausing. "There was a man that capered on knifepoints. He couldn't put a straight parting in his hair. One night in the Western Approaches, he sits up in his bunk. 'Torpedo!' he shouts. 'We're done for!' Cracks his head on the steel bulkhead and knocks himself cold."

"Were *you* scared?" the nephew asks.

"Who wasn't, that wasn't a fool? I didn't show it. You'll die if you worry, you'll die if you don't. A marinero from Newcastle told me that. He was killed off Sheerness. What's worse than any wars or bombs is to put yourself into the mouths of women."

"Listen to it!" from the kitchen.

"Almighty God, up beyond the clouds, assured your granny shortly after your birth that you would be a minister of religion. A toiler in my vineyard, was how he put it, naming you by your name and speaking Gaelic with a Carloway accent. Then, when you went off to university, we all thought you would turn out a professor. So what's leaving you in the North Sea?"

"Who knows what might happen yet, or what's in store for

him?" The home help has plunged into the room from the kitchen; blue nylon pinafore crackling, she points a reproving, yellow rubber-gloved finger at Peter. "Who knows what turn his life might take yet, when his eyes open and he puts all the foolishness of the years eaten by the locust behind him? Nothing is impossible for God to accomplish. I better get on," she says, picking up the teatray from the nephew's lap and casting an anxious glance at the window. "Listen to that wind! I saw lightning a minute ago. Was that another one?" Gripping the teatray at opposite corners, she asks the nephew, "How long are you home? Are you staying here?"

"A week. No, I'm . . ."

"Your bed's here for you."

"No, I promised friends in Harris . . ."

"Another one!" the home help exclaims anxiously. "That thunder's getting closer! Another one! Mercy on us, they're out of control altogether! And you!" negotiating a sudden bend with the teatray and rounding on Peter. "With your blasphemous, barracking tongue! A man on the lip of eternity! Have you no fear of the God who made you? Who could send a strike of lightning even now to destroy you – there's another one! – and us along with you, caught under your rooftree! Have you no fear of that? I'm not going home alone through this," she tells the nephew, as a burst of rain, on the back of the thunder, blinds the windowpane. "You'll have to convoy me."

Casting a fearful look at the ceiling, she goes into the kitchen.

"John Amos," Peter mutters into the fire. "There was another clever man that abandoned the books and went out into the world to see for himself. He died a down-and-out in Napier, New Zealand, and all the police found in his pockets was a small Gaelic New Testament his mother had given him before he left home. What does that tell an oilman with spectacles on his nose and a pen in his pocket that works? And another wild man whom I won't name from down the district never came home for years, and no one had seen hide nor hair of him, and his mother says to a young lad that's going to sea for the first time, 'If you come across my Angus on your travels,' she says, 'tell him to write to his mother,' and the young lad, who'd never clapped eyes on her Angus in his life and wouldn't know him from Jack Robinson, says 'I will'. So he's in a ship going through the Panama Canal, and a tramp steamer is in the same lock going in the opposite direction, a seaman in a holey blue jersey leaning over the stern of her, smoking, and the young lad shouts over to this seaman in Gaelic, 'Are you Angus so-and-so from Ness?' and the seaman takes the fag out of his mouth and shouts back, 'What of it?' and the young lad cups both hands round his mouth and shouts, 'Write to your mother!' What does that tell an oilman with spectacles on his nose and a pen in his pocket that works?"

"Naah!" Peter leans forward, grimacing, pulls up his trouser leg and the long john underneath, out of the bobban stocking. "Look!" reveals a perfectly round, hairless purple sausage of a leg. "The other one's worse. Soon I won't be able to manage a step."

A silence follows. Peter blinks into the fire.

"Don't want to be bedridden. Women wiping my arse for me."

He leaves the trouser leg pulled up. The nephew watches the movements of the peat fire flame. If you want to learn things, you must have patience.

"Amos, John's father . . . a dangerous man . . . he had a gun . . . once worked in the Royal in Stornoway as a barman. Your Uncle Dan was in there one Monday morning after the slaughterhouse, very quiet, when the door opens and a beautiful black Labrador appears, no collar, a length of hairy string around its neck, a Black Glen tinker on the other end of it. 'Dog all right, cof?' the tinker asks Amos. 'All right to bring the dog in, yes?' Amos studies the pair of them over the top of a glass he's polishing. 'The dog's all right' he says. '*You* can fuck off.'"

"I'm ready." The home help, wearing two headscarves under an anorak hood, small shiny black wellingtons, and with the head of a battery torch poking out of one anorak pocket, reappeared in the doorway.

"Why are you laughing?" she asked the nephew. "What's he been saying to you now? Doesn't anyone draw the curtains in here!" she exclaimed, bustling over to the window. "Allow the world to look in! I think the worst of that storm's by," she said, pulling the heavy blue curtains on their wooden rings together and arranging them so that they hung evenly. "Was that the Amos that lived at the back of Habost you were talking about? I don't remember him. He had a gun. I heard plenty about him. Why is your trouser leg like that?" she asked Peter. Kneeling on round, plump nyloned knees, she tucked the long john back into the sock and snapped the trouser leg back down, causing Peter to make a noise between a groan and a whimper. "Sssh!" she told him. Still kneeling, she looked up at the nephew and said, "Why don't you stay for a day or two? You haven't been home for ages. Keep the old grumbler company?"

"Well," the nephew started, "if I hadn't promised . . ."

"Who goes to Harris anyway? What's in Harris?"

"Well . . ." the nephew started again.

"Your bed's still here, you know. In your old room above the kitchen. Or I could make up the bed in Dan's room for you, it's warmer. Go on," she said. "Keep the old grumbler company."

The nephew looked at Peter, who was making a low whistling noise in his chest and blinking into the fire. He shrugged. "Why not?"

The home help was immediately on her feet. "I'll put you in Dan's room," she said, unbuttoning and unzipping the anorak, throwing back the hood, unknotting the headscarves and thrusting them into the anorak pocket that did not contain the battery torch. "Three things," she said, putting her anorak over the back of the sofa and sitting down to kick off her wellingtons. "Don't give him sweets. He's diabetic. Have you got sweets on you? Don't give him any. Two, don't let him sit up late watching films with naked women on the telly. And don't play cards with him. The Bard next door lost his pension to him again last week. Did I say tobacco?"

"That's four."

"He's not allowed. Listen to his chest. A single tickler could kill him. Right then," she stood up, "I'll get on. You can phone whoever it is in Harris from my house. Well," she said, ruffling the nephew's hair again and smiling down at him, "but I'm glad to see you back home, if only for a couple of days. I'm glad you're staying."

3

Uncle Dan's room, 3 a.m.: the hour when the fiend whispers. Uncle Peter, rubicund, pyjamaed, dosed with pills and a dessertspoonful of sleep-inducing jelly, is in the room below. He used to sleep across the landing, send rich snores to the rafters all night long, but can't make the stairs any more. He's awake. So much for the jelly. Now and again, he emits an uncertain series of low whistles, like a kettle starting to go on the boil, thinking about it and deciding not to bother. What is he turning over in his mind down there, at this hour? That the years, once on the rein, then on the trot, are now on the gallop? In which green or grey pasture of memory is he wandering? Or, as a bruised porridge night sky sows small needles of rain on the uncurtained windowpanes, is he out in a no man's land of the mind, indifferent, thinking of nothing at all?

The same bruised night sky sows the same small rain on the skylight up here. Nearer to God by the height of a staircase. We were never ones for shutting out the dark. The china chamberpot known as the heavy bomber is under the bed. Beside Peter's bed, in the plywood-panelled locker, is the tin one with the blue rim and handle known as the light Sussex. You didn't plan to be here. You planned to be in Harris, in Tarbert, in a three-quarter bed, with Annie Christina, spouse of Silent Sammy, who is safely offshore this week. Her pillows of bosoms bobbling both ways under the bunched orange nightdress, her rasps of heels on your buttocks... Till the dak-dak-dak and the click-click-click of feet and paws over the linoleum put an end to all, as her adenoidal lump of a four-year-old clambers damply over you to get to his mammy, and the slavering family mutt (a cross between a Rhodesian Ridgeback and a whippet) plants clumsy forepaws on your chest and exhales the offal of the ages into your face, before collapsing like a large wooden ironing board onto the bedside mat. What you get for cheating on your buddy. Well, he cheated me out of fifty quid in a boozer in Ullapool. His own fault for marrying a Skye woman. And if he finds out? He knows some nasty people. You could be a phone call away from an estate of pain and misery. A cowboy plumber has just fractured a hot pipe in my guts. What if he knows already? What if he has always known? O Jesus! That's Harris cancelled from now on. No more Macleod's Motel for you. Adulterers should be made of sterner stuff. Something, possibly a stray albatross, has just landed heavily on the slates. What if Annie Christina, that easygoing piece of Portree prime, keeps him posted on her activities, confides all into his eager Harris lug the minute he gets home? He hinted as much to you once. Heh-hehing into a pint glass the while. O Jesus!

Abandon hope of sleep for the rest of the night and put the bedside lamp on. Pink lampshade with a scalloped white fringe. Ladies' choice. You can't see Uncle Dan going into Charlie Morrison's and emerging with that. A spade, yes. Screws and brackets. Didn't Napoleon die of arsenic poisoning in a room with green wallpaper? The albatross does a two step on the roof ridge. Could read a book, there's a brown suitcaseful stowed under the bed, behind the heavy bomber. Or put Dan's dressing gown on, the one he wore in the Lewis hospital the time of his heart attack, go downstairs, make water, make tea. Peter's awake. He'll pretend he isn't.

Peter?

Waar.

Cup of tea?

Urr.

Ask him (between stentorian slurps) why his brother Dan kept to this room for the last two years of his life. Not that you'll get an answer. Why he took the family portraits and the framed Highland cow from the wall, the squares where they had hung showing lighter against the rest of the wallpaper, the hooks and roundheaded screws left in place. Why he gave the dressing table, the chest of drawers and the wardrobe to Bethesda Charity, keeping only the bedside table and lamp, a willow-pattern soup plate he used for an ashtray, an ottoman with a pink, padded lid he kept his clothes in, a suitcase of books under the bed, and a chair made in Poland. Why he appeared downstairs for meals only, not even coming downstairs to watch television in the evenings, not even for the news or if there was a football match on. He stopped reading the books, took to reading the Bible. He got rid of the sheep. He didn't fall out with Uncle Peter. He still spoke. But it wasn't conversation any more, but abrupt statements, coming from nowhere, brooking no response, or muddled rants, out of the blue, usually on politics. The rogue from down the district with the glass eye and a sinister slant, who supplied the Bard next door with cheap hooch, added a new name to his list. Solemn men with low voices, heavy overcoats, dyspepsia, talking of the means of grace and spiritual renewal, took to climbing the stairs. The day of his death was like any other. A pension Monday. Morning whitened, cold but dry. The Bard came into his door, swaying, glass in one hand, plastic bucket of salt herring in the other, shouted: "I can paddle my own fuggin canoe," went back indoors to harangue a silent television set, flail at cats that weren't there. Murdo, in the only other house on the hill, meekest of the meek, martyr to haemorrhoids, shook his head at Effie, enquired what was in the pot, *Was it fish?*, resumed his meanderings with Concordance through the hinterlands of Ezekiel. Peter shuffled between the kitchen and the scullery, kept an ear out for the horn of the baker's van, studied the instructions on a packet of paracetamol. And no clock stopped, no child's voice wailed in the firmament, no black bird of unbelievable wingspan flew over the moor, the river in the glen did not roar as though it ran with pebbles, the day the only man among them if you wanted a house built or a radio mended, a child's hair cut or a sick animal tended, closed out his term here unexpectedly, in a room bare of ornament, alone.

In that chair there, head on his chest, Bible open at Judges down one side of the chair, so that Christians and other irresponsible people could say that here was a sign. "Sign of what?" Allan Manhole (no Christian he) wants to know. "That Dan, our late neighbour and fellow-toiler in the vineyard, is to heaven gone and singing with the angels," Murdo (Church of Scotland deacon) explains. "He passed over reading from the Book. That's a sign if ever there was one." "Don't know about him singing," Allan Manhole guffaws. "*Who?* He only sang at New Year, only knew the words of one song all the way through – *Mo nighean dubh tha boidheach dubh* – and had a voice like the inside of a barrel." We're in the third house on the hill. A half-eaten clootie dumpling and a bottle of Trawler rum are on the table. And a glass of Baileys for Effie. Murdo should not be drinking black rum. "And isn't the book of Judges," Allan Manhole continued, "or am I wrong, all wars, violence and bloody murders? Visited by God's people on anyone that crossed their path? Deborah. Gideon. Samson. How's reading the book of Judges going to get Dan into Heaven by the forelock?" "You have a facetious facility in common with the rest of the fools in your family going back several generations," Murdo, meekest of the meek, martyr to haemorrhoids, informs Allan Manhole; his voice a suppressed screech. "Seed of scorpions! Brood of mockers!" "Heesht eesht eesht!" Effie, wife of Murdo, sister of Allan Manhole, soothes Murdo, who hasn't the head for strong drink. "Don't put yourself in a turmoil listening to him. And don't you dare go next door in that condition!" she warns Allan

Manhole. "And it wasn't Deborah, it was Jael." "And whereof one cannot speak, thereof one should be silent!" screeched Murdo, downing another Trawler rum in a oner. "That's in the Bible too for you!" . . . A moonspan from Eoropie to the Barvas bens later, in the kitchen next door, arms on the board, rum gone, Allan Manhole bats his bulging, hooded eyes and puts his frying pan face on Peter. "All that Heaven and Hell stuff. When I first went to sea, age sixteen, it was your brother Dan took me. As you know. It cracks my heart to think about it. He taught me splicing. Everything I know. Hauled me out of it when the little black girl in Reseef pulled up her skirt and told me it was pink inside like Princess Margaret. And I'll say this to you about your brother Dan, and so will anyone that ever sailed with him – wherever he went in the world, something happened. The world seemed to tumble out its chancers and comic singers ahead of his coming. In Liverpool, in a bar, I went up for another round, came back to the table to find him in conversation with a fellow who claimed he'd just murdered his wife in an argument over tinned peas, and couldn't think how to get rid of the body. Dan asked him where the wife was just then, and he said the spare room." Guffaw. "Another time, in Dick's on the Broomielaw . . ." Foetid night pales to clammy day, he sits on, guffawing, gesticulating; alcohol oozing from every pore in his large, globular head. Women don't want to be on their own with him, don't want him next to them on the bus. If the man whose praises you're singing was alive, you wouldn't be sitting where you are. If the man across from you was a man, he'd run you out of the house. "All right," he bawls, suddenly thumping the board, and tears start to his eyes. "So I did the dirty on him once. Let him down. Didn't he knock the seven colours of shite out of me for it at the Aird gate? So why wouldn't he forgive me after that? Why wouldn't he speak to me again? You there, Peter. Sober man. Clear-headed. Tell me." Peter puffs on his pipe, shakes his head. Says nothing.

A whinging mouth, steer it homewards. Allan Manhole stomps down the brae, feet about a yard apart, swerves in at Murdo's gate. Better a grouse landing on the windowsill. Then a teetering, two-handed grab for the doorknob. Make the brother-in-law's day. Here's my head and my feet are coming. "Is he up yet, Effie? What does he want to know about the end of the world?"

"Why did Dan and himself fall out?" you ask Peter. "Money, wasn't it?"

"What else?"

"I was only a kid."

"Cursed money. A deposit on a van. Two hundred pounds. Dan's hard-earned cash. Allan Manhole was supposed to hand it in to the garage in Stornoway."

"What happened?"

"He went to Glasgow with it."

"But he came back?"

"Two years later. In a car; a Glasgow woman driving it. My fiancée, he called her."

Silence.

"A widow. She had money. She came here, on her own, into the house, stood at the kitchen window, said poor Allan was sorry beyond the telling and offered to pay Dan back all the money he was owed. Too late for that, Dan said."

"Want more tea?"

"Naah." Groaning, he shifts his bad leg under the blankets. "These books under Dan's bed. In the suitcase. They're yours. And his American hat. What was I saying?"

"Allan Manhole."

Peter laughs.

"In less than a week, after telling the world he's going to settle here, do up his grandfather's house in Lionel, he's back on the mainland, car, widow and all. In less than a month, he's back on the island, no car, no widow, and no shoes on his feet coming down the gangplank of the Loch Seaforth. Where do you stay yourself when you're not on an oilrig in the North Sea?"

"Here and there. Glasgow, mainly."

"When I was on ships, I made myself familiar with every bolt and rivet on them, from stem to stern. In case of emergency. I hope you're the same. Tell me now. Where are all the pressure points on this oilrig of yours?"

"It isn't an oilrig. It's a platform."

He's watching me. I shake my head. Silence.

"Do you still see the children? They'll be grown up now."

"When I can, yes."

"What about your wife?"

"Not really. She's married again."

"She still sends me a Christmas card . . . Why don't you come back here, stay here?" he asks, after another long silence. "I'll soon be gone, you know."

"Bullshit!"

"He's come away from the clothes pole. He's on the door mat. You should come home."

"To *Ness*?" Appear to consider it, finger tapping on chin, eyes ceilingwards. Regretfully shake head.

"Maybe someday." Laugh a laugh. "Some yellow Mayday."

"There are worse places in the world," Peter says. "I've been there, I've seen them. It's your house," he says. "Dan put it in your name."

"I know." Stand up. "I'll think about it. Well," you say, "but look at the time."

"She still displays a shapely calf."

"Who? Give us that cup there."

"Big Joan."

(The home help)

"Big handsome woman. You could do worse, you know."

"She's nine years *older* than me, for Christ's sake!"

"So? She's still a fine-looking woman. And you'd have two houses and three crofts between you."

"Why are you looking at women's legs, at your age?"

In Boulogne, a mademoiselle sat on his knee, put her arms around his neck. He was in naval uniform. He sang her a Gaelic song. She kissed him, all over his face and neck, even his eyes, wet smacking kisses. No end to them.

"Right," you say, "I'm going to bed."

"Remember to say your prayers. You believe in God, don't you?"

Believe in the God of Israel, of Moses and the prophets, who sent his Son, begotten of Virgin, to earth, that we might inherit eternal life. Swallow that whopper whole. The Gaelic and English bibles of my youth, rotted and mildewed, spines broken, pages torn, are stuffed under the stairs; not one of them ever thrown out. Ask him does he believe in God himself? at the age of eighty-five, has he seen the light? Not that you'll get an answer. Through slits of eyes watching me. The last of the Mohicans.

"I don't *have* a home," you tell him. "And you'll live to be a hundred. You'll get your picture in the *Stornoway Gazette*, cutting a cake, and a telegram from the Queen of England."

4

The book at arm's length, Uncle Dan still couldn't make out the words. "Go and get eyeglasses", Uncle Peter told him. "There's a man on a corner in Stornoway, name of Banks." But he wouldn't.

"Here!" Handing you the blue-covered *Poems and Songs of Robert Burns*, that had been all round the world with him, that fell into the dock in Chittagong and was rescued by a black man in a punt.

"Which one tonight?"

"To a Louse. On Seeing One on a Lady's Bonnet in Church". Page one hundred and thirty-seven.

He sat back happily, folded his arms. Peter, in his chair at the other side of the fire, removed the pipe from his mouth, prepared to listen.

Haw, where ye gaun, ye crawlin ferlie . . .

"Ferlie," said Peter.

Dan looked narrowly at him.

"What's a ferlie?"

"A flea!" Dan shouted. "A louse! A flea! Now can we hear the rest of it without interruptions?"

The books in the suitcase under the bed used to be on shelves in a wall press on Uncle Dan's side of the living room fire. The door of the wall press had a pearl grey knob that came away in your hand; dark brown holes above and below the knob, where it had formerly been screwed into the wood and failed to take a purchase.

Not all of the books in the press were Uncle Dan's. Some belonged to Aunty Katag. *Sparks from the Anvil. The Heavenly Footman*, by John Bunyan, translated into Gaelic. *Spiritual Songs*, by Rev. Peter Grant, Strathspey. *Sguaban Bhoais. Thoughts upon the Gospels*, by Rev. I. D. Macdonald, M.A., Kilwinning, formerly Ferintosh. Written on the flyleaf of *A Call to the Unconverted*: Miss C. Morrison, 7 Hughenden Drive, Glasgow W.2. 25 May, 1948. 7 Hughenden Drive was a surgeon's house. Aunty Katag was the cook there.

Uncle Dan never read any of Aunty Katag's books. Nor did he persist, beyond the title page, with *Hygiene for Nurses, Dorlach Sil, The Works of Josephus, The Days of the Fathers in Ross-shire, Needlecraft Made Easy, Teach Yourself Rugmaking, Shag the Caribou* or *A Pictorial Guide to Flower Arranging*.

Grasping a rafter in the barn from beneath with the fingertips of his right hand, he pulls himself up so that his head is level with the beam. Drops back to the floor, light as a cat. Murdo Dan Balallan, who has notions about himself, eyes the rafter tentatively. Looks at Dan. Dan grins at him.

"You can do it!"

He can't. No one can. Except maybe a Russian gymnast.

"You're not normal, you damn freak," Murdo Dan Balallan tells Dan. He looks up at the rafter. "Bugger off!" he says.

Peter plods in out of the fine rain, puffing, selects a swede turnip for the Sunday dinner from the mound in the corner. Murdo Dan Balallan leaps on Dan from behind and puts a stranglehold on him.

"Right," Murdo Dan Balallan tells Dan. "Say you're sorry."

Dan bends down low, bowing under the weight. Murdo Dan Balallan clings to his back, feet off the ground, maintaining the half-nelson. Peter plods out again, carrying the swede by its top. He doesn't speak. How can brothers be so unalike?

"Ask him is he sorry?" Murdo Dan Balallan says. "A nod will do."

Squatting, you peer into Dan's face.

The face, a big grin on it, looks out at you. Nods.

"Is he submitting?"

The face nods.

"And will he never give me a red face again?"

Dan suddenly pivots, breaks Murdo Dan Balallan's hold and puts him on his back on the floor of the barn. Murdo Dan Balallan looks up at him.

"You big bully!"

"That'll bother him now for the rest of the day," Dan says, when Murdo Dan Balallan departs. He rubs his palms together, they rasp like sandpaper; his voice softens almost to a whisper. "Ah, but you should have seen me one time. Before the years put their hobble and halter on me. What a man I was then!"

"Were you in a lot of fights? I heard you were."

"I never started a fight in my life. Who told you that?"

"What about the twins?"

"No," he shook his head. "They had one another. They were identical, you know. Separate, you couldn't tell which one was which. Together, you could, because Peter was smaller. No," he shook his head again, "they trotted about in a world of their own, populated by teddy bears and a black doll called Susan and a strange pal from Fivepenny who used to come and stay with them on the holidays. They never fought anyone."

"What fights did *you* have?"

"Not even in the wee school. Me? I never started a fight in my life. I finished them. You wouldn't have wanted to take me on."

He stared out at the rain.

"One morning, in the public bar of the Royal in Stornoway,

I took on four tinkers. An argument over a dog, caused by Amos the barman, who spent the entire fight dodging behind the counter, brandishing a mop. Hard men, the four of them, they gave as good as they got, and I was eighteen years of age. But I put them out. I made them scatter. I'll tell you something else, before we go for another load. That was the morning I found out what cut of a man I was. To know that you won't back off from anyone or anything – that's a great thing to know. To be unafraid, whatever comes. Let it come. Face it. Why be afraid? I never felt more alive, more clear-headed, more sure of myself, than I did that morning. Not even in the war. There's the rain off." He stopped in the doorway and said in the same soft voice, "They couldn't beat me. I could have taken on a dozen, the strength that was in me then. I could have fought forever. How could they beat me?"

He climbed into the seat of the grey tractor, which roared and spat out a frantic plume of black smoke, which turned pale blue and then grey before vanishing to nothing in the watery light. You climbed into the trailer, held on to the high, slatted wooden side with both hands. The tractor roared again, disgorging another plume of greyish blue smoke. Uncle Dan turned his head and grinned. In Tamburlaine's sandshoes, Alexander the Great's donkey-jacket, Field Marshal Montgomery's beret slanted jauntily across your brow, you take a triumphal ride the length of the district. To fetch a load of sand from Traigh Shanndaidh in Eoropie.

Upstairs again, you pull the large brown suitcase out from under the bed. It's heavy. You need both hands. Two locks. Like the cases Indian pedlars used to haul from house to house back in the 1950s, rain or no rain. Remember them on the Mitchell bus. Pakistanis, too. Their cases blocking the passageway, making an obstacle course for the drinkers in the back seats who needed to stop the bus in the Barvas moor to go out for a piss.

Open it. It isn't locked.

You won't sleep again now.

Could go a drink. *God grant those drunkards drink that wake at dawn.* How Lowry felt. There isn't a drop in the house. Not even a quarter bottle of Martell brandy for medicinal purposes . . .

> *As once more through the window they espy,*
> *Looming, the frightful Pontefract of day . . .*

Adam Bede isn't in the suitcase. The Shakespeare with the cut pages is. "Ah, but!" said Uncle Dan. "Falstaff didn't run away like the others. He tried one or two swipes with the sword first before he legged it."

He preferred Hotspur to Henry the Fourth. When Owen Glendower said he could call spirits from the vasty deep:

> *Why, so can I and so can any man*
> *But will they come when you do call for them?*

Where's The Vicar of Wakefield?

"Now that you've succeeded in locating the house, explain this to me."

It's Friday night. He's in his chair by the fire. The sleeves of the tartan working shirt are rolled up to the elbows. But even inside the house, the shirt collar stays buttoned.

"A sheep out on the ben I can see so clear, I could almost tell you the markings on her from my own doorway. That tanker today on the horizon heading north was a Norwegian. But put a newspaper under my nose and I'm blind as a mole. What do you think?" reaching into the press and taking a fat book in a soft red leather cover from the bottom shelf.

You turn the book over in your hand. It's Friday night. You're home from school in Stornoway for the weekend. There's a dance in the ATC hut in Adabrock. You only called in on the uncles to see how they were and get a lend of Dan's bicycle.

The Pickwick Papers. By Charles Dickens.

"Read where they go shooting with Mr Pickwick in the wheelbarrow," Dan urges. "It's only eight o'clock. Mr. Winkle in the witness box. Anywhere you like."

At eleven o'clock, you rise to go.

"Dances in Ness never start properly before midnight," Dan reassures you. "Unless they've changed considerably since my day, when we used to dance on the Dell bridge till morning to one melodeon. Well, but I wonder how Mr Jingle and Job Trotter got on in Australia. A pair of rascals. But you can't help laughing."

He'd washed his hair with green household soap in a basin in the scullery, and it was standing straight up.

"Katy Mary Hannah," Peter says, "sent her dancing shoes to a shop in Glasgow to be mended. They came back with a ticket on them: *Beyond repair.*"

"Where are you working now?" you ask Dan.

He's a stonemason. His palms, when he rubs them together, make a noise like sandpaper.

"Galson. Blockwork," he adds disgustedly. "A child could do it."

The Dickens is part of a set. Illustrations by Cruickshank. Some you like better than others. Barnaby Rudge, no. Uncle Dan tells you there was a hat in his granny's day called the Dolly Varden. It had a feather in it. You read *Kidnapped* together. "A lean, mean, shifty bugger," he says of Uncle Ebenezer. "Gets his comeuppance in the end, though . . ."

When Mr Shuan murders Ransome the cabin boy, his fists clenched, the sinews in his forearms convulsed and tightened under the black hair, and he muttered fiercely under his breath:

"Never mind, never mind. He'll be meeting his own stag any minute."

(Meaning Alan Breck.)

"There was a man for you!" he exclaimed. "He was a real man, you know. Stevenson didn't make him up. John Roy Stewart. He raised a regiment in Edinburgh for the Prince, and fought at the head of them on the left of the front line at Culloden. Latha Chulfhodair. He made two poems about it. Where's Sar Obair nam Bard?" He dived into the press, rummaged among the heavier books, found the *Beauties of Gaelic Poetry* in its brown paper cover. "He's in here. Iain Ruadh Stiubhart. Towards the end of the book . . ."

"But I can't read Gaelic."

"Ah, no. No. Well," he muttered rapidly, averting his eyes, "never mind, never mind."

And closing the *Beauties of Gaelic Poetry*, put it gently back on its shelf.

5

The bus laboured up the last rise before Stornoway, and there, in a field on the left hand side, all on its own, was the sign: Rowat's Tea. "Stornoway Big of the Castle", a large, gaunt sailor with a yellow face and wild brown eyes in the seat behind you loudly informed the rest of the passengers. "What's the time on Syme's clock? Eleven ack emma, ding dong. Let all the bolts on all the doors of all the public houses in town commence their screeching." "Amen agus amen," a voice beside him croaked, through cigarette smoke. The voice of his crony. "Here!" The large sailor's grey bristly jaw, mouthful of tawny, blackened teeth, breath that could knock over an elephant, thrust itself between Uncle Peter's head and yours; a terrible hand claps Peter on the shoulder. "Going up to the hospital to see Dan, aren't you? I heard he was taken in. Heart attack, was it? How's he doing? Tell him Dodo was asking for him." "And The Catfish," the voice in the smoke croaked. "Tell him The Catfish was asking does he remember an eighty foot rip in Galveston?"

They came off the bus at the Mac's Imperial. "Do you know The Catfish?" The large sailor poked the nephew jovially between the ribs. "This is The Catfish."

"Hello."

"How's she logging?"

"Still play poker, you fat robber?" the large sailor asked Peter. "Come down to Swainbost for a game sometime. We're loaded. See if you can take it off us."

After buying large oranges in Capaldi's, and a tin of Crawford's assorted biscuits in Woolies, Peter wondered out loud:

"Will we go up there straight away, or to Caberelli's first for a cup of tea?"

"Go up now," the nephew said. "Get it over."

Three days since Dan was taken into hospital. Three days and a night. Peter has been to see him twice. This is the nephew's first time. He hates hospitals.

On the night of his heart attack, in the kitchen, he told the two ambulancemen who appeared with a stretcher and a blanket to wrap round him: "I'll walk out of the house on my own two feet, boys."

And to Peter, who had put on his good tweed jacket and bonnet and proper shoes: "You stay put. Look after the livestock."

Inside the holdall the nephew is carrying are a change of underclothes and a new dressing gown and pyjamas and slippers bought by Aunty Ishbel in Murdo Maclean's. They find him in a bedside chair in a bright, sunlit ward, wearing a hospital dressing gown and slippers and reading *Little Dorrit*.

"Where'd you get the Gregories?" the nephew asked, in a mock-hearty voice, smiling. Dan took the glasses off. He didn't smile back.

"They're mine," a man in the next bed replied. He sat up, causing the bed to creak. He was a fat man with a flattened nose, eyes like a spaniel dog's and black hair plastered severely across his skull. "From Bragar, boys," he told them, speaking in a languid, vowel-lengthening drawl. "You're lucky you caught me. I'm going home any minute." He turned his head towards the door of the ward and concentrated hard. Reassured that no one was listening, he looked sadly at the nephew and confided:

"That beetch of a nurse from Carloway never stops pestering me. 'Sit up and take an interest!' 'Look out of the window!' 'Eat that banana your daughter brought you!' 'Shaddab, you beetch,' I said to her. 'Why should I sit up, or eat a banana, or look at black cows in a field, when my feet are pointed towards eternity?'"

An odd expression came on his face, as though his mouth had filled with water; he lay down, causing the bed to creak again, and turned his back on them. From the movement of his shoulders, he seemed to be weeping quietly. The nephew looked at Dan. Dan shook his head.

The third occupant of the ward, a small chubby man with a woolmat of frizzy, wavy grey hair haloing his head, now rose from his supine position on top of the bed in the corner, slid along the polished floor on leather slippers that were too big for him, halted by the fat man's bed, said "At it again!" and after convulsively wrapping the blue and white striped hospital dressing gown round himself, arrived at the foot of Uncle Dan's bed and fixed Peter with small bright eyes, red-rimmed and lashless, like a bird's. "Are you related to the Dooleys?" he asked Peter, taking his bottom false teeth out and retaining them in his hand. "You look like Murdo George Dooley. Anything on you?" he asked. "No?" He looked at the nephew. "Don't listen to a word that fellow says," he said, pointing at the fat man's back. "He's never been anywhere. Doctors?" He turned to Peter. "Have you seen the doctors in this place? They have plastic cards on their pullovers with their names on them. They don't wear white coats. Dr Macfarlane. Dr Levison. And Dr Alex John Babaloola. Which one have I got?" His voice rose peevishly. "Dr Alex John Babaloola! I don't understand a word he says. I try to answer his questions. Everything he puts on me. But I can't. How can I answer when I don't understand the question?" He waved the hand holding the false teeth. "Graham there gets Dr Macfarlane. So does Dan. Are you his relations? But I get Dr Alex John Babaloola. Anything on the hip?" he asked the nephew. "Vodka? I'll drink anything." He stood with his red-rimmed, lashless eyes, staring at nothing. "They give me a white pill, like a pandrop, three times a day. Crushed in a spoon with water. The nurse gives it to me. She's from Carloway." He stared some more. "Bermuda," he said. "That's where I'm going when I get out of here. I've got contacts there. Anyone you know in Bermuda, say the word. I'll look them up for you." When next he spoke, it wasn't to either of them, but to an imaginary small creature perched on his left shoulder, that no one could see but himself. "Not one word Dr Alex John Babloola says do I understand," he told this creature. "I don't understand one word Dr Alex John Babaloola says. When I try to answer, he rolls his eyes around in his head and bares his teeth at me. You'd think he was back in the jungle. Everyone else in here . . ." he waved the hand holding the false teeth, ". . . gets a proper doctor. But I get an African savage."

"Where's he from?" the nephew whispered, as the small chubby man, dressing gown flapping, slid on leather soles back down the ward, pausing at the end of the fat man's bed to hiss viciously: "She's coming! She's here!" Uncle Dan, who had put the glasses back on and continued to read *Little Dorrit* all through the small man's harangue, raised his head, removed the glasses, and frowned.

"South Lochs," he said.

Through the ward window, the sun flew over sombre evergreens and the asphalt square and cream-pillared iron gates at the hospital entrance. Slates and windows of grey council houses across the road, wet after rain, scintillated in sudden light; behind them, undulating at the limits of the town, green fields rejoiced, waved to children to come and play on them. The wheel come round, a glad young world astir – Uncle Dan's face hung blankly over his book. The man from Bragar kept his face to the wall. The man from South Lochs stared up at the ceiling.

6

The waiting room at Aberdeen heliport is small, smoke-laden, overcrowded. The floor is on two levels. On the lower level is the check-in desk, worked by a fat cheerful girl in a blue uniform and spectacles, who seems to know everybody, and a thin man, also in uniform, whose main function is to record the weight of the luggage. Hovering importantly behind them, the brick-red face, flopping jowls and large ginger moustache of the Controller of Flights. There are chairs and tables all round the walls, and at this hour of the morning – 7 a.m. – all the chairs are occupied by men waiting to go out on the rigs. Men are sitting on the tables, on suitcases, on the floor and on the four steps that lead to the upper level. The upper level has a tea and coffee bar, which also sells milk, soft drinks, sandwiches, chewing gum, hot pies and sausage rolls (not at the moment) newspapers (sometimes) and soft porn (always). Above the continual babble of voices – up here also is crowded – two other noises intrude all the time – the noise of the glass double doors at the main entrance opening and shutting as more and more men arrive to check in, and the high, prolonged squeal of the door of the men's toilet, on its airlock device, at the far end of the tea and coffee bar.

The nephew is in a chair at a table on the lower level, eyes closed, feet crossed at the ankles and planted on a holdall. Voices of his fellow crew members come and go all round him, heard on the borders of consciousness, between sleep and waking.

". . . no, yih, but you must know old Bill, yih, old Bill Youngson, Bella's husband, Christ, Bella from the Criterion, when old whatshisname hed the Criterion, old George Low, yih?"

". . . that arsehole with the Battle of Britain moustache has his eye on Charlie. He won't let you on board the chopper if he thinks you're drunk, that ginger arsehole."

". . . We hed some nights in there, I tell you. My oath! Old George Low. He was . . . yih, he . . . always wore a spotted bow tie, old George. Dead now. Snuffed it. And old . . . Christ! Old Endrew! Bloody old Endrew!"

". . . fa, Norman, he'll be a' richt, nevvar worry. So onywye he comes over, ken, an' grabs us . . . I'm at the bar, ken, same as here with you . . ."

"Ah'm no' gaun. Cannae face it, Tam. That rig flair. Smell of diesel. American accents . . ."

"Date of arrival on rig . . . What's the date, coz?"

". . . ken the wye them Scousars spik, canna mak' head nor tail of them half the time, woa ay aye, he says, oo's fookin' startin' he says . . ."

"After you with the biro, Rich. 'e's got bugger all in his pockets but bookies' dockets and breadcrumbs . . ."

"He got the nick. Month, two month ago, in Aberdeen. Breach of the peace, assault. Outside the Anchorage."

"Fuck a wild man!"

"Six month he got, was it?"

"Fuck a nine-year-old fat boy!"

"Wint after a boy outside the Anchorage, did he?"

"Howya goin' thar, Rich? Hey! Whar's ole Bobby at?"

The nephew opens his eyes, yawns behind his hand, sits up, looks at Rich (fellow floorman) and then at his watch. Ten past seven. He rubs the window beside him, which is running with condensation, and looks out, his nose flattened against the glass, hands cupped against the sides of his head to shut out the yellow neon light of the waiting room. A dull, flat morning. On one of the helipads, a British Airways helicopter is revving up, its main rotary blades a smooth, blurred circle of speed against the indifferent light; tail rotor a white wheel. Behind it, another helicopter is being refuelled by three mechanics in white boilersuits. Further out, another helicopter, red and white navigation lights flashing, turns and manoeuvres into position on the runway.

He settles back in his seat again. Puts his feet back on the holdall. A history of waiting in waiting rooms. Train stations. Ferry terminals. For the train just departed, the boat newly embarked. Not this morning, though.

"Feeling rough, coz?"

"Lousy."

"Want a coffee?"

"No thanks, Rich. I'll wait till the rig."

Pulls a face, closes his eyes.

The voice of the girl at the check-in desk erupts over the loudspeaker system. Startled, he opens his eyes.

"Would all members of Zephyr 1 crew please report to checkout immediately All members of Zephyr 1 crew to checkout immediately."

He yawns again, and consults a blackboard on the wall behind the weighing machine, which lists this morning's flight times:

0700 Pacesetter 1

0715 Ocean Victory.

0715 Zephyr 1

0730 Piper "A"

0745 Sedco 700

0800 Transocean Conqueror.

The first two flights listed have already gone – a chalk line has been drawn through them.

The crew of Zephyr 1 start filing through a doorway to the left of the check-in desk. At a long zinc counter behind the door, Customs and Security men are waiting to check their bags. Tom, Kiwi and Rich, who have been standing, find seats at a table newly vacated by the Zephyr 1 crew.

Aberdeen's orange glow rising. You lived there once, many moons ago, knew your way around, the lie of the boozers. Knew other times, in other waiting rooms. A woman who had been punched holding a bloody cloth to her mouth. A boy, a child, retrieving her false teeth from the floor for her. We'll get married then, he told the girl called Victoria. Not if you don't want to. Sure I want to. Sitting with a poker up his arse in the Social Security office, Gallowgate, he quite fancied the prospect of becoming a father. I'll get a job, he said. She looked at him. Doing what? Anything. I've a pair of hands, haven't

I? I'm not forcing you, you know. Her eyes on him: green. His mother said: "You're not bringing that lowland whore up here." She wrote: "You have brought my grey hairs in sorrow to the grave." She bawled: "Stop drooling over that cot with your drunken breath and go and look for a job. It's Victoria I feel sorry for . . ."

Vicky of the Egyptian eyes, open-toed sandals, roll your own fags, shouldering to and fro in a two-room rented flat. Bog on the landing, meter in the press. He lullabied a baby, their third. *Toora loora loora. Toora loora lai.* Doomed for a certain time to walk the night. Behind him, in the half-dark, Vicky, meant for better things, moaned, stretched out a shapely arm, drank water from a glass. Settled again.

> "*. . . hush now, don't you cry*
> *Toora loora loora . . .*"

After the break-up, what did he do? Where did he go? Corby, London, Jersey, London, Kettering, Glasgow, Dublin, Aberdeen. Sick and weak from the drink, huddling his misery in the blue morning heliport, an oilworker now, boy. He went to Harris, after all. Large Oklahoman Indian driller beside him contemplates the Departures board, despatches a gob of tobacco juice phut-ping into a metal bucket, drawls: "Look like they're really gonna send us out there, Slim." And what news of the ex-wife? Vicky, you mean? Oh, she went back to university, learned to drive, dyed her hair, joined an amateur dramatic society, took guitar lessons, graduated, remarried, the minute my back was turned. The children are fine too. The third one – the insomniac – is now in secondary school.

> "*. . . you go your way*
> *and I'll go mine*
> *now and forever till . . .*"

"Shee-it!" said the big Oklahoman, when their flight was called over the tannoy.

"Here we go, Slim," he said.

Follow the crew, carrying their bags, through the doorway to the left of the check-in desk. Your helicopter on the other side of the plate glass window, seen through your reflection in the plate glass window, in close, near the edge of the tarmac. Charlie, the crane operator, points:

"There she is. The paraffin budgie."

Two customs men. Open your bag for the skinny one. He rootles among the contents in correct training manual manner. Nothing in there to make your day. The noise of the helicopter, loud and relentless, coming through the open glass door, at the far end of the counter, that leads out to the runways. "B" Crew, Piper "A", stand in line. You know them all. They have lives ashore, homes, wives, children, parents, brothers, sisters, relatives in the next county, girlfriends, dogs, ex-wives, football teams, publicans, probation officers, bookmakers, best friends, blackmailers, assorted bastards in bulk and Inland Revenue officials making demands on them. Names. Bill, Reid, Sandy, Tom, Billy, Charlie, Richie, Norman, Kiwi, Freddie, Mick from the Rebel County and Yorky, who has women in three different cities in the north of England. *Though they sleep, yet they shall waken. When He sends His fire over the face of the waters. And they shall walk in the midst of the burning; and not a hair on their heads shall be singed.*

"OK, coz?" Richie asks.

Grins at you. From Sunderland, and sees the moves. What it is to be a strong man with an easy temper.

Move out through the open door and across the concrete forecourt to where the helicopter is. Round to the front, following the neck of Freddie, the roustabout, and hand your clean-of-contraband bag to the man on duty at the loading bay. Above your head, the great whirl of the main rotary blades; in your nostrils, the hot, sweet stench of high-octane fuel; in your ears, the deafening roar of the engines. Follow the bell-bottomed denims of Freddie up the rickety folding steps of the aircraft; both of you (hungover) clutching the vibrating metal handrail. You are last but one to board the helicopter. Last is Bill Deer, toolpusher, Oklahoma Indian and boss of the bunch.

Have to get into these awkward bloody orange survival suits laid out on each seat. Then tie the black bag containing an inflatable safety jacket around your waist. Sit beside Richie, and tell yourself, swallowing hard, that the nausea brought on by all that exertion will go away. One of the pilots comes up the passageway. Tailing him, the simian, white-boilersuited figure of the man who was stowing the luggage. So wide he has to move along the passage sideways. The man leaves. The pilot pulls the door shut from the inside after him. Comes back to the front of the helicopter, stands there holding the bag containing a lifejacket.

"Good morning, gentlemen. Have you all flown in a helicopter before? Has anyone *not* flown in a helicopter before? Good. All know how to operate a safety jacket? Anyone *not* know how to operate a safety jacket? Good."

He goes through the uncurtained cabin doorway, sits in the left hand seat. The other pilot can be seen checking and re-checking the switches, dials, red and green winking lights on the instrument panel before him. The first pilot addresses them through the intercom:

". . . behalf of Captain Davies and myself . . . welcome you aboard the British Airways Sikorsky 21 helicopter . . ."

Sandy, from the front seat, shouts up to Norman:

"Borrow one of your papers?"

"Fit?"

". . . flying time out to the rig this morning . . . approximately an hour and twenty minutes . . ."

"*Pay*-pars! *News*paypars!"

". . . seat belts . . . securely fastened . . ."

"Hinna read it yet!"

". . . all smoking materials . . . extinguished . . ."

"Canna hear you!"

"Hinna read it masel'!"

". . . Thank you."

Beside you, Richie settles himself more comfortably, closes his eyes.

"Givvus a shout when we get to the rig, coz."

The helicopter moves forward slowly along the runway. Stops. Your Uncle Peter is dying. You couldn't stay with him. Two days you managed. Then you ran for your life. To another man's woman in Harris. To a trail of bars. Seated at the window beside Richie, you watch the dirty bleached grass at the edge of the runway blown back and flattened by the windstream from the blades. Freddy has already burrowed down in his seat and closed his eyes. Tom and Kiwi are reading newspapers. Norman, face thrust forward between the seats, is talking rapidly to Mick and Yorky, sitting in front of him. In front of them, sitting perfectly still, Bill Deer. At the very front, Reid and Sandy also sit quietly, doing nothing at all.

The pilot in the right hand seat reaches for a lever above his head. The noise of the engines rises to a shrieking pitch that drowns all conversation, and the helicopter, throbbing and shaking in every component, seems to raise itself slightly, as though on stilts, poised and straining for flight. The pilot holds his arm steady on the overhead lever for five seconds, then, almost imperceptibly, the helicopter rises; the concrete runway, the windblown grass strips in between, steadily falling away, tilting, as the helicopter, still gaining height, leans smoothly to port, the engines now giving out a muted, staccato barking, as though a machine gun were rapidly puttering overhead; then, as the helicopter tilts further, the airport buildings, the hangars, the helipads with "H" printed on them in white capitals, suddenly appear below, minute at this height and at strange, foreshortened angles, then, the ploughed parklands beyond the heliport, and the lights, misty-yellow in the distance, of Aberdeen airport, and the blue runways, and the rain-silvered morning roofs of Dyce, while all the time, through the windows on the starboard side, the low winter sky, dirty with clouds, slants by unchecked. The red "No

Smoking/Fasten Seat Belts' sign above the door goes out. Still making his sweep to starboard, gaining height all the time, the pilot heads her north-north east, out towards the sea.

7

Every summer, at the start of the holidays, the nephew goes to Ness to stay with his uncles, Dan and Peter.

When he first started going, he had to stay with Aunty Ishbel and Murdo her husband in their house at the upper end of the village. There, he had to come in early at night, go to bed with daylight still on the windows, and take baths. But once he reached the age of ten, he was allowed to stay with the uncles.

Uncle Dan was the elder, by three years. He did the outside work. He had sheep and cows and two crofts – one at the west end of the village – Number 6 – separated from Aunty Ishbel's and Murdo's by boundary stones, and the big family croft – Number 34 – at the east end of the village, near the river. He was a stonemason and builder of drystone dykes, and it was said of him that he never refused a stone; that she was still rumbling in the bowels of Vesuvius, the stone that would defy him to find a place for her. He was tall and thin and unbelievably strong, with a lean, boney face, a nose carrying a white scar across from a fight on a Mayday hire, fierce black eyebrows and a prominent Adam's apple. Viewed from the side, with a plumed hat on his head, he would have resembled the Duke of Wellington. He wore a tartan working shirt with the top collar button always closed, under a bobban gansey, under a blue lybro bib dungaree; a Harris tweed cap on his head and black size eight wellingtons with the tops folded down on his feet. When he shaved on Saturday nights in the small mirror in the scullery window, he used a cutthroat razor which he carefully wetted beforehand on a special small oilstone. He didn't like safety razors. He didn't like shaving.

Uncle Peter kept the house, did the cooking, and dealt with the vans that came round during the week, blaring their horns – the baker on Mondays, Donald Duncan on Wednesdays, Alickan on Fridays and the butcher on Saturdays. Cupping the creased leather purse with the housekeeping in his left hand, he would reluctantly undo the clasp and poke around in it with the index finger of his right hand, disturbing the coins but not removing any. "How much?" he would ask, suspiciously eyeing Donald Duncan, and when Donald Duncan confirmed the figure – "Have you gone mad? Has greed finally deprived you of the last remnants of shame and decency? Give the boy a sweet," he would say then, and to the boy, "Don't bother with a sticky one. Get one that'll keep you sucking for a while."

The uncles were not famous for getting up early. Peter was first to rise. From his bed in the small room with the skylight above the kitchen, the nephew would hear him puffing downstairs in his stocking soles, speaking to Sheila the dog and opening the front door to let in the cats. After that would come the dull clang of the Rayburn door opening, a brief but furious rattling at the damper, and Peter, in his slippers, shuffling out to the dungheap behind the house with the ashbox. The fire in the Rayburn, smoored with heavy peat overnight, would still be red – they only let the fire out once a year, the day they cleaned the chimney – Uncle Dan aloft, at the lum, with the brushes and the long rope with the weights and bunch of barbed wire attached, Uncle Peter below, at the sootbox, eyes narrowed, cheeks puffed out in apprehension, holding a potato sack at arm's length, waiting. The kettle would be on the boil, the porridge pot bubbling, the frying pan sounding like the sea going back down a pebbly beach, before the next creak on the staircase alerted the nephew that Uncle Dan was on the move, and that he might as well get up himself, to save Uncle Peter banging on the ceiling from below with the head of the sweeping brush.

After breakfast, if there was enough water in the river, the nephew would go out to collect worms, turning over the stones that had fallen from the walls of the old house. Back indoors to fetch his folding rod, he would also collect the sandwiches, wrapped in greaseproof paper, that Peter had made for him, from the top of the dresser. Quite often, a banana or an orange would be with them. "So where are you going to try today?" Uncle Dan, at the head of the table, with Sheila the dog by his side, would ask. "Now if I was you, on a day like this, I wouldn't put a hook in the water until I reached the Grey Knolls – the big pool at the

Grey Knolls. Start fishing from there. That's what I'd do if I was you."

Uncle Dan was a sailor when he was young. He was all over the world. He was up in Murmansk, in Russia, and he met a fellow from Lochs there, and he was down near Cape Horn, in a place called Punto Arenas, and he met a fellow from Lochs there, too. "Wherever you go in this world, you'll meet one," Uncle Peter said. "I bumped into one myself in Alexandria – a fellow from Rainis." And where was Alexandria, and what was Uncle Peter doing there? In Egypt, in the navy. During the war. "There's me in the navy," he said, removing a snapshot from the shortbread tin with Stirling Castle on the lid. "Look how skinny I was in those days!" "Calum Spoke met a man from Lochs in Honolulu!" Uncle Dan said. "Working in a bar with girls in grass skirts and palm trees. He was wearing a bow tie."

Peter put the shortbread tin with the photographs back under the television table. "Well," he said, standing up, "but I better do a bit of polishing and dusting before sister Ishbel appears." Starting at one end of the mantelpiece, he blew on the large Bible with the names of the family in it, on the sailing ship in the bottle, on the threepenny stamp with the head of King George VI, on the Smiths clock that imitated Big Ben and only needed winding once a fortnight, on the brown and white envelopes behind the clock, on the glass duck – a mallard – that Wee Annie Nicholson gave to their mother before she went away to Canada, on the jamjar of sixpences, on the tobacco pouch and knife, and on the three washers, the small bottle of iodine and the box of Swan Vestas at the other end. Straightening, he blew, above the mantelpiece, on the portrait of his father and mother, on the picture of HMS Vigilant, and on the small framed photograph of Wee Donald, their brother and Peter's twin, who died of pneumonia in Portsmouth, aged nineteen. "That's better," he said, settling himself again in the soft leather armchair with the fat arms and taking his pipe from his trouser pocket. "Let her start a row now, if she likes."

Uncle Dan and the nephew worked all afternoon at the hay on the family croft. At half past six, they went home for their tea.

A smell of frying chops and onions met them in the door of the scullery. The kitchen quivered with heat; you couldn't see out of the windows for steam. On a high, three-legged stool in front of the

Rayburn, uncle Peter was slicing the peeled cold potatoes left over from dinner into the frying pan. "Are you starving?" he asked the nephew. "Say yes."

"Did the paper come?" Uncle Dan asked.

"Yes."

"Is it the right one? He didn't leave the Record again?"

"I never looked."

Up in the livingroom after tea, uncle Dan rolled a tickler, lit it, shook open his newspaper and angled it to catch the evening light from the window behind him.

"A glance at world affairs," he said, "before we go to the park for the cows."

"Remember Sportscene is on the telly tonight," uncle Peter reminded them. "At 10.20."

He lit his pipe with a match from the Swan Vestas box. The match burned down to the tops of his fingers before she went out. He didn't seem to notice.

"Murdo was rockfishing last night," he said. "At Idhinis. He caught plenty."

"We'll go tomorrow night, if you like," Uncle Dan told the nephew. "What do you say?"

"You bet."

"He'll need a white fly," said Uncle Peter.

"So make him one," said Uncle Dan. "You're the man with the knowhow."

The blue cat called Archie climbed into Peter's lap, started walking on him with his front legs, purring loudly, without moving from the spot.

"Stop putting the claws in me," Peter told him. "Stop it, I said!" *He didn't put Archie back on the floor.*

"And this Friday," said Uncle Dan, "if we're both alive and kicking, we'll go over to Goathill to watch Ness knock spots off the Stornoway Athletics."

The nephew likes staying with his uncles – Uncle Dan and Uncle Peter. There is nothing in the world he likes better.

He'll be with them this summer again.

Instead of going home after the match, the three westsiders went to the Eoropie bothan. They stood in the mouth of the doorway, filling the doorway, and the Nessmen inside told them to come in and shifted up to make room for them. Side by side on a bench, with round red faces and plump hands folded over round bellies, they resembled three Buddhas sitting in a row. They drank whisky with beer chasers, and when the whisky ran out, black rum; and admitted, when it was put to them in the course of the evening, that Ness were the better team. One had round wire glasses; another a gansey with a high neck and zip. They stayed in the bothan till morning and were no trouble at all. They were quiet men. The one with the wire glasses bought a raffle ticket for a ram from Jojo.

As This Leaves Me

Viewed from the air, the first three houses in the east end of the village form an isosceles triangle. At the base of the triangle beside the main road, are Kenneth's house – Taigh a' Ghlinne – in the glen, and my house – River View – further uphill. At the apex almost out in the moor, is Malky's house, that used to be called Babsag's. Malky isn't there any more and in the paper last week I saw, with no surprise, that that house is now for sale.

Kenneth came out today; I was glad. I happened to be at the scullery window at the time and there he was, in the front door, in the blue nylon boiler suit and the black leather slippers with the holes cut in them to let his bunions breathe. He suffers with bunions, always has; his mother's fault for keeping him in shoes too small when he was in primary school. (A woman famous for meanness, like all her people; her brother in Port used to go to the fish van and buy one kipper.) Out he came, the first time for weeks, and up the road a little way, head down, and no daylight showing between the soles of his slippers and the surface of the road; then about turn and back down the road, into the house. I never went out to speak to him. What could I have said? Even if I'd been out when he appeared, I wouldn't have known what to say, beyond acknowledging the day. And if I'd been out, he probably wouldn't have come out in the first place.

No sooner is he back indoors than the phone rings in here. It's John Doogie's wife, across the road. "Did you see what I just saw?" she starts – no hello or anything. "I couldn't believe my eyes! I said to John, 'Come here John,' I said, 'and tell me my eyes are not deceiving me. Of course *he* didn't shift . . ." I let her rattle along like that for a minute or two, then I said, "Sorry to interrupt you, Margaret, but I've got to go, there's a pan of potatoes spilling over on the stove," and hung up. It is essential to have let-outs like that whenever someone like John Doogie's wife comes on the phone. Another one I have is, "The cat's up on the ornaments again." With my sister in Melbost, it's "There's someone at the front door," adding, "a Jehovah's Witness, from the look of him," in case she tells me to never mind the door and listen to what she's saying. I can't use that one on Margaret Doogie, she's across the road from me and sees my every move.

It couldn't have been easy for him. The whole village knew what was going on. The whole district. The poor fool who's married to her is the last to know what his wife's like – personal experience talking here. And when the poor fool is told what's going on and then refuses to believe it? – personal experience talking again, with some difficulty, through a whistling gap in his upper gum where three front teeth used to be. Never go between a man and his wife. That's the eleventh commandment. Or between two tinkers. I'm not saying Kenneth was stupid. But he acted as if he was. As a school boy, he was always the one being sent for spirit levels with no bubbles and tins of tartan paint by the older boys. And he happily carried this pretend innocence and gullibility with him into his adult years. It isn't such a bad ploy, after all, for getting through life. He seemed to trust everyone; believe everything he was told. And if something turned out to be not true, that didn't matter. He never bore grudges. I never heard him raise his voice in anger. His world was straight out of the large picture books we used to get as children from the lady missionary – peopled with loving parents, faithful friends, good neighbours, wise teachers, godly ministers, honest thieves and whores with hearts of gold. What else? I don't know. It would be easier to describe the dark side of the moon. The thing is that until the Italian woman came along, there was nothing much to say about him. He was good on the melodeon and at singing. Children were fond of him and he was fond of them; they were forever following him about, in and out of his loom shed, and he never told them to be quiet or go away and always spoke to them as if they were adults. He cleaned the village chimneys. He could advise a woman with a load of washing if it was going to rain or not; his bunions, he claimed, acted as barometers. And he couldn't drown kittens or train sheepdogs. On fank days, he had to keep his dog on a leash, in case it got among the sheep the other dogs had rounded up and scattered them. When the other men made fun of him for this, Kenneth laughed along with them. "God knows who you belong to!" his father, a saturnine, emaciated weaver who suffered from constipation, shot out at him one New Year's morning (the house full of people at the time) and Kenneth – plump-cheeked, snub-nosed, bald from alopecia at twenty five apart from a sparse ginger fuzz above the ears and around the back of his head – nodded placidly in the silence that followed, as if to say, *I quite agree with you.*

Until the Italian woman came along he was like everyone else in the village. No particular attention was paid to him. After the Italian woman all that changed; and nothing here will ever be the same again.

Our family has always lived in this village. Both my brothers have houses here – John in the west end (grand-uncle William's croft) and William down in Lochside. As the eldest, I have the family home. No one lives with me. I was married twice, but they're both long gone. One couldn't stand the prospect of spending the rest of her life so far from a Marks & Spencer's, and the other couldn't stand me. That isn't as facetious as it sounds – my first wife, on her departure for the mainland, left me with over a thousand pounds of debt to mail order catalogues to remember her by. "Look at you," my slattern of a second wife would shrill at me, cigarette smoke issuing from her nostrils, as with dustpan and brush I followed her spoor across the living room, "You're picking crumbs off the carpet and the sky is falling!" She was from the mainland, too. But this story isn't about me and my wives.

When Kenneth left the local junior secondary school, he did what most other boys from the district did who weren't in the big school in Stornoway or apprenticed to a trade, or shortsighted, or colourblind – he went to sea. This was when Britain still had a merchant navy. Two other lads from the village went to sea with him – Babsag's son, Malcolm, known as Malky (his father was a butcher's son from Perth, according to the other girls from Ness who were in the hotel with Babsag) and my own brother William. Malky did one trip as a deck boy to Canada on a ship of the Donaldson Line, then came ashore for keeps, not saying anything about his experience. My brother William became a captain with Denholms, and after that on cruise liners. Kenneth sailed for years as an able seaman with the old New Zealand Shipping Company, leaving home in October after the harvest was done, and coming back in April when the spring work was starting. The tropical sun that tanned other seamen's faces turned Kenneth's a flaky, freckled pink. Over the years my brother used to try and persuade him to leave the New Zealand Shipping Company and come and sail with himself, but he wouldn't do it. He was happy where he was.

Then his father died (of an apoplectic fit, in the back of Panny's tractor, among sacks of potatoes) and he had to give up the sea in order to look after his mother, who couldn't be trusted in the house on her own. It was a happy time in Taigh a' Ghlinne. His mother's absentmindedness wasn't a great problem at the beginning, she could get about perfectly well, go visiting on her own and go out to the different vans that stopped at the house, so long as Kenneth left a line and a purse with money on the scullery windowsill for her. One Saturday I went in to a great smell of baking and Kenneth kneading dough in a big, yellow baking bowl – his mother was showing him how to make floury scones. "From the hand of a master baker!" he shouted, offering me one on a wire rack, and not at all embarrassed. Another time – an evening – I found them sitting across from one another at the kitchen table, his mother with her hand cupped behind her ear and tears in her eyes as Kenneth, holding his own ear and also on the verge of tears, sang a dirge for her from a small notebook he carried about with him. They were fine.

So, there he was, back home all the time, going around and about in a blue seaman's cap and wellingtons with the tops turned down and his hands in his pockets, and I suggested to him that he might become a weaver. He looked blankly at me when I said it.

"After all," I continued – we were in my house at the time, at the living room table – "there's a perfectly good loom of your father's sitting idle in the shed."

He kept looking at me.

"Do you know," he said finally, slowly, "that never entered my head. That's a good idea."

"Better than spending your life, day in day out, with a straw in the corner of your mouth, blathering to children."

"You're right . . ."

"Wandering the shoreline, singing to yourself."

"I'll do it." He stood up. "Good thinking, kimosabby."

"About these . . ." With a sweep of my hand that covered half the table, I indicated the scatter of forms, final demands and threatening letters from the Inland Revenue that he'd brought for my perusal, "I'll need all your payslips from the company for the past few years."

"Payslips?" The blank look came back on his face.

"Payslips," I repeated. "Every time you're paid off from a ship, you would have received a payslip or statement, telling how much you'd earned, how much was deducted and so on."

"Oh yes."

"You kept them, I hope?"

His face went pink. He looked like a schoolboy being asked why he hadn't handed in his ink exercise.

"Well . . . no."

"Why not?"

"Was I *supposed* to . . . ?"

"We'll write to the Company, they'll have kept your records." I stood up, and we went back down to the kitchen, where Malky was sitting at the table demonstrating to my second wife how easy it was to roll your own cigarettes. Two high, red spots had come out on my wife's cheeks, a sure sign she was enjoying herself. Malky sat back in his chair when we appeared, but didn't stand up. "Well?" he grinned at Kenneth. "Did the scholar make head or tail of it?"

"Let's go," Kenneth said to him.

"I'll never manage it," my wife told Malky, crumpling a Rizla cigarette paper and shreds of Golden Virginia tobacco between her fingers. She looked up at us and gave a small laugh.

"You keep these, Fiona." Malky pushed the four rollups he'd already made across the formica to her, closed his tobacco tin and put it in his breastpocket. "Don't let the bodach smoke them on you." This was a joke, as everyone knows I don't smoke. My wife laughed.

"Are you coming?" Kenneth asked him, from the door.

"I am." Grinning, he got to his feet and hobbled across the kitchen, toes turned inwards, imitating Kenneth's walk. I could smell the drink on him as he went past me. Kenneth and my wife laughed. Kenneth had been drinking, too. It was a Saturday afternoon. I watched them go down the path and along the road to Kenneth's house.

"He's nice," my wife's voice said at my shoulder.

"Who?"

"Who do you think? The big one!"

They wouldn't be going into the house, where the mother was. They'd be going into the shed, where the bottle was.

"He's not that much bigger."

"Yes he is." My wife lit one of Malky's rollups and started sucking on it.

"They look the same size to me."

[46]

"Well, he seems bigger. Anyway, he's nice. Friendly. You know. Fun. Remember fun?"

She blew smoke out loudly through her nostrils. Tickled me with a finger under the ear.

"Can't you use an ashtray?" I said.

"Why will the other one never sit down if I'm there?" she wondered out loud.

"Will he not?"

"You know he won't. Even if he accepts a cup of tea, he'll drink it standing at the Rayburn. Smiling his weird smile and shifting his feet. What's wrong with him, anyway?"

"Told you," I said. They'd gone round the back of the house and into the shed. I turned to my wife then, and noted with pleasure that Malky's rollup had gone out, and that tar from the end of the rollup had stained her lower lip dark brown on one side.

"Maybe you make him nervous," I said.

My brother William was born in this house. John and I were sent across the road to Doogie's house, and I remember Doogie's girls at the window, jumping up and down and screeching, and when we went to have a look – all except John Doogie – my father was in the door, waving us to come over, so we did – all except John Doogie – and here was a baby that didn't have a name yet going *waa* and Doogie's girls all got to hold him. Two days later, on our way home from school, we were shouted into The Goat's house – The Goat was Kenneth's father's nickname – and when we all went in – all except John Doogie – here was another baby with bright red hair, fast asleep, and we all got a sixpence and a slice of gingerbread, and this was Kenneth. Before the month was out, Babsag paused from scrubbing the potatoes for dinner in her Auntie Marion's house in Lochside and casually dropped Malky on the linoleum floor of the scullery. So, three boys were born in this village in the space of a month – there wasn't a month between them

[47]

– and you would look far and travel further to find a more unlikely trio.

Perhaps it was entering the world so precipitately, or bad blood on the Perth butcher's side, or his docile drudge of a mother – everybody's servant – denying him nothing, stirring his tea for him and tying his shoelaces, that fixed a petulant scowl on Malky's face from childhood and kept him aloof in boyhood from the other two; a lone loiterer with a panoply of social graces that included the torturing of cats and flies, the setting on fire of tar barrels and haystacks, the breaking of church windows, the breaking of cups on telegraph poles, the discharging of an air pistol at old women on their way to church, and the attempted rape of John T.'s middle daughter, Little Flossie, when he was still in primary school. Add to these a propensity for hitting his mother with fists and feet if she ventured an opinion that didn't accord with his own, or if his tea wasn't ready on time, or she was slow in giving him money, and you begin to see the young Malky plain. "He'll do for you one of these days," John T. raged up at her, when he came over from Aird to, as he put it himself, make a football of Malky's head his feet would never dribble. (Babsag had locked the doors against him and was shouting from a skylight that no one was going to lay a finger on her boy). "You didn't learn him at the knee, and you won't learn him at the shoulder! Now let me in and let me at him!" John T. spoke nothing but the truth. Home after his single trip to sea, Malky flung a heavy pair of scissors at Babsag one afternoon that speared her in the back of the thigh. "That's how Davy Crockett did it!" he shouted. Unable to staunch the bleeding, and carrying a small suitcase, Babsag hobbled the length of the village to her Auntie Marion's house in Lochside as soon as night fell and stayed there ever after, leaving Malky, aged seventeen, in sole possession of the house in the east end and its contents. Once he'd sobered up, he went to Auntie Marion's to fetch his mother back, but she wouldn't go with him. She was afraid for her life. Auntie Marion, who wasn't slack ("A child with eyes that don't incline my heart to gladness has come into our family," she told my mother) chased him; and when he came back a second time, looking for money this time, she put the police on him. Interchangeable sluts from Stornoway, full of booze, bad language and belligerence, a mad woman from the mainland who tried to drown herself in the river (choosing for her purpose a pool that wasn't a foot deep), and a fat nurse from Harris with the largest breasts I have ever seen and a Mini Austin that Malky ran over the breakwater in Port, were the only females who stayed in Babsag's house thereafter, and none of them stayed longer than a weekend. Local girls never went there. They knew what a bad bastard he was.

Everyone has good points. A saving grace. Some redeeming quality. Even Hitler had a soft spot for animals and children. So what are Malky's good points? Thinking hard while the clock ticks the world away I tried to recall a child on whom Malky pressed a caramel toffee, a dotard for whom Malky carried home the messages, an animal from whose paw Malky removed a thorn. I can't think of any.

When my brother William, the last of the trio, was five years old he told his sister, two years older than him, not to make a noise drinking her soup – an early conversation-stopper from someone destined to instruct and command his fellow-creatures. Seven years older, I took him by the hand to school on his first day. We had to walk to school then, a distance of a mile and a half – my brother John took Kenneth, who was wearing a tartan tie and had a schoolbag on his back wider than his shoulders, and Babsag took Malky. On their road home in the afternoon – the infants were released earlier than us – Malky started to bully Kenneth as soon as they were out of sight of the houses. Kenneth offered no resistance. Bored at last with hitting someone who merely crouched against the dyke of the Mill park with his arms across his eyes and wouldn't start crying or run away, Malky then turned his attentions on my brother William. It was a mistake.

The tinkers who had been in the Brae quarry all summer were still there in August. They saw the fight that followed and one of them, Old Joseph, came to see my father.

"I've seen many sights and spectacles in my time, Angus, with these old eyes," he said, slapping his hat against his leg. "But never before this day a child that fights like a grown man."

My father frowned at him.

"What are you on about?"

"Your boy!" Old Joseph exclaimed in a kind of rapture. "Your young one!"

"Go inside," my father told me. I did, but only as far as the rainwater barrel.

"My word," Old Joseph continued, "but the Irishman got it right when he said the sword isn't as terrible as the fire in the eye of the one that wields it." With that, he threw his hat on the ground, spat on his hands, adopted a fighting stance and started to show my father what he, Joseph, with his old eyes had seen his, my father's, young one doing to the whelp with the everlasting frown belonging to the black one out in the moor, Allan John's daughter, and what, before that, he had seen the whelp of the black one out in the moor, who didn't resemble his late godly grandfather Allan John in any way, doing to the Little Red Bagman, as he'd already dubbed Kenneth.

"Come in, Joseph," my father said. I dodged in smartly ahead of them. Old Joseph was a holy man, a patriarch of the travelling people, honoured wherever he went. He didn't behave like a holy man. ("We're travelling people, boys, not tinkers," he told us one night when we were in the quarry listening to Black Alex John on the bagpipes.) My father picked up his hat from the ground and handed it to him. Old Joseph put it back on his head, but took it off again in the doorway.

"O spread Thy covering wings around, till all our wanderings cease!" he declaimed to my mother. "I've come to shake the hand of the future flyweight champion of the world. Is he in the house?"

"Who's he talking about?" my mother asked.

"William," my father said.

"Change his name to Alexander," Old Joseph said.

"He's upstairs," my mother said.

"Won't you sit down?" she said to Old Joseph. To me, she said: "Go and get your brother." To my father: "What's he done, anyway?" To Old Joseph: "You'll have a cup of tea." To me: "Are you still standing there?"

But when I went upstairs to fetch William, he was nowhere to be found. What he did, I discovered afterwards, was position himself beside the bedroom door, so that the door, opening inwards, hid him from view and the room seemed to be empty. He was full of tricks like that. My father, steeping his feet in a basin of water in front of the fire one time, made the mistake of asking William to bring more hot water from one of the kettles on the kitchen stove. William appeared, cheeks puffed out, carefully holding the handle of the kettle in both hands with a dishtowel. Just before he reached my father, he pretended to trip and flung the kettle into my father's lap. My father, leaping up, knocked over the chair and the basin, roaring and bawling that he was burnt alive, before he realised that the kettle contained cold water.

"And do you know this?" Old Joseph was saying when I came back downstairs – his hat now on the floor of the kitchen – "Once the fight is over, I see him talking to the sullen one to make him stop crying, then to the Little Red Bagman, who'd started crying because the sullen one was crying, and he makes him stop as well. And the last I see is the three of them going down the Mill brae together, quite happy, the wars over and done with, your fellow in the middle."

"I'll give him wars when I catch him," my mother said. "His first day in school!"

"No, you won't, Jessie," Old Joseph counselled her. "You

won't utter one word to that boy." He picked up his teacup, then put it down again.

"God be with the children!" he suddenly cried, shaking his head and a sob came into his voice. "God take them under the shadow of His wing, keep and protect them from the snares and tribulations of this world. Bad days are coming. Jehovah hear them in the day when trouble He dost send! Strengthen them against the bad days that are coming!" I didn't wait to hear any more. At the first mention of God's name I was sidestepping along the wall of the kitchen towards the scullery door and the front door and the wide world beyond. It's the only thing to do when Christians start. Don't bother to make your excuses. Just get to hell out of it.

Known as a clever family ("They're a clever family") my brother John and my sister and I all passed the qualifying examination in primary school and went to the senior secondary school in Stornoway where we stayed in hostels in the town for six long years and only came home every second weekend. In this way I lost touch with my youngest brother, although I never paid much attention to him anyway; the gap in years between us saw to that. I was aware of him around and about the house, always with his pal Kenneth in tow. Once, I came on the pair of them in the barn, a bicycle they were constructing on its back between them, studying a steel rod with a bolt attached to it, that Kenneth had in his hand; another time, they went missing on the moor, but turned up with a bag full of trout just before a search party consisting of my father and The Goat and two dogs set off to look for them. But any contact I had with them usually consisted of a knuckle-rap on the head if either one came near me. I was big, they were small. It was the done thing.

William, too, passed the qualifying exam in primary school, and that was when he made his first big move. Told by Soapy, the headmaster – pen poised confidently over the form – that he would be going to the senior secondary school in Stornoway, like his brothers and his sister before him, William replied that he wouldn't; that, on the contrary, he would be going to the junior secondary school in Lionel. He gave the same answer to his father and mother, and to anyone else who tried to reason or remonstrate with him.

"How come?" I asked the top of his head.

He looked up.

"What?"

"You're not going to school in Stornoway?" I was in university, I was grown up. I had a moustache, a motorbike, a girlfriend. I was in a position to advise him.

He shook his head and went back to the book he was reading.

"Come on!" I chaffed him in a manly, mock-hearty voice. "Surely you want an education?"

"Not there," he said

"Why?"

He shook his head again.

"Speak!" I commanded him. "Speak or I'll give you a knocker."

He looked up.

"It wouldn't be any use to me," he said.

"So according to you," I couldn't believe I was having this conversation, "taking out an education is a waste of time?"

"I didn't say that."

"I'm wasting my time. That's what you're saying."

"No."

"It's what you're implying."

"You're you," he said.

"What do you mean?"

"You're doing what's right for *you*," he explained reasonably, keeping a finger on his place in the book, and looking up at me as though *I* were the twelve-year-old and dim to boot. "What you think is right for *you*. It wouldn't be right for me."

"How do you know that? At *your* age?"

"I've thought about it," he said, and added, as if to reassure me, "I know what I'm doing."

[53]

"Do you?"

"Yes."

He removed his finger and started reading again. I stood over him. I felt foolish. There didn't seem to be anything more to say. He sat reading. I felt like hitting him.

"What's that? A Western?"

I snatched the book roughly from his hand and turned it over.

"*A History of Scotland*," I read. "Good, is it?"

"It's all right."

"Good, is it? Who gave it to you?"

"Grand-uncle William."

"Yeah, well. And it's good, you say?"

"It's all right."

He held out his hand.

"Can I have it back now?" he said.

In order for this story to go forward, I now have to go back over my own fouled-up life and career. I graduated from Glasgow University with an honours degree in history in 1966 – the year England won the World Cup – and after a year at Jordanhill College of Education, I started teaching in Hamilton Academy, Lanarkshire, and also got married. She was a small, plump, cheerful girl, my first wife, who couldn't pass a paper clip on the pavement without wanting to pick it up. For six months we lived in Meadow Road, Partick, then we moved to Atholl Gardens, Hillhead, and looking back to that time it seems to me that we were happy, that I was happy. We had two girls, Maggie and Kate, and I used to stand with them in my arms at the great bay window of the flat on summer evenings and watch the elm tree outside the window cast its flowers in the wind, and the laburnum flowers falling in the gardens below, on the other side of the road. Saturdays, we would wheel the babies down to the shops – Kate in the pram, Maggie in a seat on top of the pram carriage – and Glasgow and Gaelic drunks on Byres Road would sway over them, make emotional, nonsensical speeches and give them money. Sometimes, my brother John, who had started going to the dogs, would be among them. But he never came to visit us. Three years went by. I had bought a ground floor flat on White Street, Partick. One afternoon I came back from Hamilton early, let myself into the flat: no noise of children, no sign of my wife – where were they? I was filling a kettle at the kitchen tap when I heard a noise behind me and, turning, saw my wife coming out of the bedroom in her dressing gown, followed by my brother John with a look of impudent innocence on his face. "Sorry about this," he mumbled, and lurched into the doorpost on his way out. I packed a suitcase the same afternoon and took a taxi to Central Station. I had no idea where I was going. I went to London. A fellow from our village – James Murray – a big shot in the Civil Service, was down there and doing well for himself. We were the same age and had been rivals all through school. He put me up for a week, in a house he'd newly bought in Ealing. I drank every day and talked to him at night. I kept him from his bed. He put up with it for a week. The last night I was there, I took a woman back with me. In the morning, he threw the woman out, sat me down at the kitchen table (which he always set for breakfast the night before), gave me a hair of the dog and told me to go back home to my wife and children. He saw me off at King's Cross. I think he wanted to make sure I got on the train. I was a bit crazy at the time. He was glad to see the back of me. Later, when I was myself again, I wrote him a letter, thanking him for his hospitality, but he never replied.

Back in Partick, in the house that is no longer a home, the woman taken in adultery wails, wrings her hands, and her nose turns bright red with contrition. Three more years passed. We're still together. We barely speak. There's another child, another girl. By 1974, I'm teaching in Harris. I watched the 1974 World Cup final in a windy, carpetless house in the Bays. Peat smoke from an old Modern Mistress stove fills the room. From the previous owner we have also inherited

a framed picture, *When Did You Last See Your Father?*, a
one-eyed cat, a cracked sewage pipe and fleas. All night the
house creaks and cracks; in the chimneys, live creatures scuffle
and fall heavily. Children cry. A job comes up in Stornoway.
I take it. We move into one half of this house. My parents
are in the other half. My father dies. My wife and my mother
cannot live together. My mother, loudly bemoaning the evil
days that are in it for her at the end of her days, goes to live
with my auntie in Melbost. My sister, on her holidays from
the Western Infirmary, stays there as well, and where tell me
is brother John all this time? No one knows. For seven years,
not a sight, not a sign. Then, after seven years, like a human
locust, he turns up on grand-uncle Williams's doorstep one
night, a holdall made in Ireland in one hand, a case of whisky
in the other. For a holiday, he said. He's there to this day.
He's there as I write. We never speak. His gross wife filled
my doorway one morning at the end of last year, overflowed
into the scullery – thank God, she didn't come further – and
burbled something about Christmas dinner, would I, their
house, brothers after all, family, shame, please come. I told
her to take herself and her invitations and her fat arse out of
it, only I didn't say fat arse as the hands on her can make fists
and do, from time to time I'm happy to hear, on brother John's
person. So I confined myself to telling her that celebrating an
unholy, alien festival over a groaning board with her haggard
fornicator of a husband was not especially to my taste and fancy
– no offence to yourself, Johnina, I hurriedly added – and she
seemed to accept this, merely batting her tiny cavewoman's
eyes twice at me, before swaying out and allowing the scullery
to fill up with daylight again.

Having the free run of the house she always wanted doesn't
make my first wife any more settled. This bloody village, she
keeps saying. This bloody island. This bloody life. Leafing a
Kays or John Noble catalogue with the girls, she exclaims over
clothes, footwear, crockery, food mixers. Isn't that lovely! That
would suit *you*, Kate! "Have they done their homework?" I

ventured to enquire, concerned father. They stare at me. She stares at me. "Give me one good reason why I should stay any longer in this misery," she says. You don't want me to stay. I don't want me to stay. So why should I stay? And back with her to Glasgow and the warren of relatives she has there. I don't care. I've got a girlfriend, an academic from the Lothians with long legs and four or five languages. "Certainly, we're going to be married," she tells me, crossing the long legs. She has a rented house in Laxdale. "You don't think I'm going to live in sin with you in Ness, do you? My God!" During the act of sexual congress, she sounds like a gaggle of roosting fowls sensing the presence of a mink in the henhouse. How can my small, croupy cockadoodledoos compete with this? Also, she writes Gaelic poetry that doesn't rhyme or scan or make sense. These are considerations that need to be mulled over with a clear head. Only someone utterly careless of his own continuing wellbeing would ignore them. If that's what you want, I say. Also, she smokes like a Buckie trawler. On the wedding night, she slides her back down the wall of the hotel room, sits on the floor, chin on knees, eyes dead. Order another bottle of champagne, she orders. Start as you mean to go on. Not that she's a drinker. She works in the local college, and for different Gaelic organisations, acronyms, bodies involved with the language; attends seminars, conferences, gatherings of Gaels from the four quarters of the globe. She's a spokesperson, a visiting lecturer, a poet, a neutral observer. Not having the language is a decided advantage when making a career in Gaelic arts or education. Back in the village, she won't permit anyone to speak to her in English. "Speak Gaelic!" she orders. When she speaks Gaelic herself, brows furrow, eyes go round, jaws sag, the angel of silence descends. No children, no time for that. Saving the ancient language of the Gael comes first. Chained to such an extravagant creature, it isn't long before I make the acquaintance of other stirks and asses, all, like herself, from the south, all her dear best friends, all speaking Gaelic out of notebooks, dictionaries, grammar books, and all gainfully employed in the Gaelic "world". They write poetry as well, these friends, sometimes together, in alternating couplets, in climbing boots, going up hills, and having no gift for language or talent for writing doesn't seem to deter them. Sometimes they read this poetry out loud in public places, to meagre audiences of white settlers and the odd Gaelic-speaking fool, usually very old, who feels for some reason that such people should be encouraged. They dress rather elaborately for these occasions – one with a carefully tended six days' growth of beard and blue spectacles, transforms himself into a Buchan ploughman; another bloodless bastard, also bespectacled, becomes Aubrey Beardsley; a hiccupy female academic from Perth with teeth and a face full of broken veins favours a shiny red velvet trouser suit and mediaeval buskins laced with hairy twine – and afterwards they all come back here. I sit in my father's armchair, watching them. Who are these people? Where have they come from? Why are they in my house? Among her manifold accomplishments, the academic makes her own wine. She has brought some along, chinking in a bag. Do have some. Oh, no thanks, I'll stick to whisky. Oh, go on. Oh no really. Grape and the grain, you know. Oh, come on. Oh, leave him be, my wife interrupts. All the more for ourselves. Poised in the centre of the living room after a glass or three of it, she recites her latest poem; raises her arms above her head, revealing the coarse black hair under each armpit. It is a poem about love and the death of love and feelings. The lady speaks in Welsh. My Gaelic – fluent, idiomatic, Lewis – has no place in this company of outlandish babblers. It is dying the death in a small room, my Gaelic. A language gets the devotees it deserves. Neglect something and you'll lose it. And wheresoever the corpse is, there shall the vultures gather.

Not that I don't already have my suspicions about this mouthy, multilingual bitch who insisted on marrying me. We go a jaunt to Paris for a week, and with French coming at us from all angles, she barely opens her mouth. I think to hell with this, and fuelled by the wine of the country, start blathering in my own execrable school French to barmen, street Arabs, waitresses in cafés, sellers of tickets and balloons and any other citizen who happens to stray within earshot. This makes my wife very unhappy. For God's sake shut up! she orders. To hell with that. By the end of the week I'm going great guns; in one shop, under my own steam, I manage to buy a hat and a French World Cup scarf from two attractive girl assistants. They laugh a lot all through the transaction, encourage Monsieur l' Ecosse to keep talking Français, tell me I have a great look of Michel Platini, adjust the *chapeau* at different angles on my head, escort me, giggling, to the door. This makes my wife very unhappy.

Back home again, my wife employs a painter and decorator – Malky, no less – on a long-term contract. Can he lay carpets as well? Of course, he can. He can do anything. This ugly old house is going to get a major overhaul. Just you wait! Malky and my wife pore over samples of curtain material, con books of wallpaper patterns. A tractor comes to the house in my absence and all my poor old mother's furniture, except the Welsh dresser, is thrown into the back of a trailer and driven to the district dump. English scavengers remove it from there before I can organise a salvage operation. Then vans driven by boilersuited Stornoway coves appear, laden with new furniture from over the sea. Blond wood, very Scandinavian, very expensive. My arse aches. The family portraits are down. Modern prints in severe frames take their place. Was she expected to sit under my great grandmother's frown for the rest of her life? Malky has done the bedroom upstairs and the landing. I should get the house rewired, he now tells me. He'll do it. And downstairs, underneath the bath, he suspects dry rot. From the sour-faced, uncommunicative drunkard I have always known, Malky has blossomed into a grinning and at times most voluble Jack-of-all-trades. It must be the small fortune my wife is giving him. She's in charge of the joint account and all our finances. Jabbering in English, they hold their daily conference at the white pine kitchen table. More and more money is needed. A major plumbing job is on the cards. Malky can do that, too. He employs Kenneth for a fortnight as a labourer. I point out that commencing with the interior decoration and then working back to the carpentry and plumbing, whilst unusual and innovative, is not the established way of doing things in the construction industry. They stare at me. She stares at me. I need more space in my life, she says, and you are violating the little space I have. I can't breathe. Would you mind moving into the spare room upstairs for a while? And then into the spare room downstairs, once Malcolm is finished in there? On the white pine chair at the white pine table, a plate of microwaved supermarket Chicken Kiev and oven chips in front of me, I absently agree, thinking the while of salt herring and potatoes boiled in their jackets, plates of mutton broth, barley bread, dumplings. Saliva fills my mouth and tears start to my eyes. Oh God! she exclaims, what's wrong with you *now*? What do you ever do in bed anyway but fart, snore and pick your nose in your sleep? And, anyway, she continues, these feelings of mine could be *temporary*. Don't you know *anything* about women? When Malky, after dismantling the hired scaffolding from the chimneyhead, wondered aloud whether we wanted a new cement path and pavement all round the house, seeing he still had the use of the mixer, I called a halt to his activities. My wife wasn't pleased.

"Oh, I *see*," she says. "I'm supposed to break an ankle or worse on that obstacle course you call a path, just because you're too mean to part with a little money?"

"Little!" I protested. "I've parted with thousands!"

"And not before time! This place was a *tip* before I came!" She has a trick, when arguing, of prodding the middle air with the forefinger of the hand not holding a cigarette. Mimicking my voice – a grotesque noise – she pursues me through the house and traps me in the downstairs lavatory, where I have retreated for safety.

"Well?" she shouts. "What do I tell Malcolm? He's waiting!" I must get a snib for the door of the downstairs lavatory. This marriage is not happy.

"Anything you like," I say.

For weeks after that, the put-put-put of Malky's mixer dins in my early-morning ears. Kenneth is re-hired. His seaman's cap turned around on his head, I watch him, in a violent gale of raining wind, laying slabs of yellow sandstone on a mixture of sand and cement, underlaid with polythene sheeting, at the front of the house. What is this? It's a patio! Every house at the Butt of Lewis should have one! What does she have in mind next? A ballroom extension? A pagoda? I go to my brother William's house in Lochside to tell him my woes. I'm drunk. I wipe my feet before entering. Captain Bill is back from a long trick to tropical climes. His wife went with him. The captain's lady, Katie Ann. She shows me a piece of coral and a wood carving of a tropical fish. She shows me a photograph of the black man who carved the fish. He offered her cannabis. He called it ganja. She nearly took it, just to try it. Captain Bill indulgently shakes his head. Make him tea, he says. They have no children, Captain Bill and his wife. One of brother John's boys, who is staying over, slopes in from the computer room. Through the door he left open, I see rows of screens, some with moving images; I see red and green buttons of light. I hear electronic noises. It's the bridge of the Starship Enterprise in there. Captain Bill, brows already corrugating in concentration rises from his chair and preceded by the youth, goes out to deal with the aberration thrown up by one of the computers. The door closes behind them. Katie Ann fills my teacup with whisky, the minute his back is turned.

"Bugger it," she says, and pours a splash into her own.

"Why did you marry that sanctimonious shit?" I ask her.

"Money and travel," she replies.

"I should have married your sister Catherine."

"Too late now."

You should only love the unattainable. Get any closer, you'll get your heart broken. "She's blown the joint account," I tell William. "All my hard-earned cash. Now I find she's been keeping a separate account for herself." He doesn't say anything. He lets me talk. I'm slurring my words and not making sense. This is the effect he has on me. What did I ever do to deserve such a brother? For the tramp who ruined my first marriage, he buys tractors, explains politics. I stop talking and he looks at me, expressionless.

"How are your girls?" he asks. "Are they coming home this summer? When did you see them?"

Once he retires from sea, he'll be a district councillor, a deacon, and then an elder in the Free Church, and I wouldn't bet against him becoming a lay preacher either. The spiritual reference books and concordances jostle one another on the shelves; the little brown Sustentation Fund envelopes are on the windowsill, awaiting the Sabbath. *Daily Readings From The Bible*, by Spurgeon, a volume you would need both hands to lift, has a tasselled bookcard marking the place for today's morning reading (over) and today's evening reading (to come). Has he ever been drunk? Woken up not knowing where or with whom? Spent money he shouldn't have? A heavy hard cover Gaelic Bible, *From Father to William*, puts to sea with him every trip, has done since he was sixteen. Handy for clobbering mutinous wee Filipino stewards on the bonce. One wallop from the family Bible, and a ganglion of mine on the back of my left hand, vanished forever, never to return. Who says God isn't good? I arise to go. My children are fine, I reassure no one, and write faithfully every week of their crowded lives to dad, small "d". For some reason, this triggers a speech.

"When married couples part," he censoriously groans, "there is anger, there is hatred, there is apportioning of blame. But these feelings are not permanent and do not last. And as your eye at that time should have been on those mistakes you made in the past, for which, as I recall clearly, you did not seek either God's forgiveness or your then-wife's, so your eye, now, should be on making acknowledgement to God and your now-wife of those mistakes you have made, and guarding against similar mistakes in future."

Well, fuck me with a ragman's bugle! A good job I came here tonight! And here's to the history of Scotland! Now go and dance the reel of Tulloch, you pontificating prick! . . . Great news! I tell the Medusa of the pumicestone pan when I reel in some hours later and find her still up, hair hissing, waiting for me. She has great news for me, too. She's leaving. Her bags, her boxes, her matching suitcases, her steamer trunks are packed and ready for the convoy of removal vans to come and carry them away. Ordering me into a fashionable wooden chair with arms, she proceeds to make the longest speech since Cicero was in his heyday. Torrential Edinburgh English hurls interrogation points at the stippled ceiling, peppers with exclamation marks the wallpapered walls. Twice I interrupt her in order to go for a piss and recirculate the blood to my numbed buttocks, but she follows me, still orating, into the as yet unsnibbed downstairs bathroom. Well? she demands to know as a weak dawn insinuates itself through a chink in the fashionable, blue-green drapes. I shrug, extend my hands, palms upward – a Gallic gesture of resignation, acceptance. Is that it? she wants to know. I hang my head, clasp my knees with my hands – Rodin's *Thinker* on the lavatory, sang dumb. Right! she snorts, and stomps off to bed, trailing a hail of punctuation behind her. Farewell to Nova Scotia!

All this was four years ago. She took off for the Isle of Skye and the Gaelic college there, and I haven't seen hide nor hair of her since; nor have I heard her voice on the telephone, nor have I read a line of her writing. As though she'd never been. The same with the one in Glasgow. The children, for a long time now, have been at an age where they could travel up here by themselves to see their dad, small "d", but somehow this has not happened. There is a legal arrangement whereby money for the upbringing of the children is deducted from my pay every month, and I speak to them on the telephone on Sunday mornings if they're at home and remember their birthdays and Christmas, and write short letters to them, to which, sometimes, they reply. What more can I do? If they want to see me, they know where I am. I would pay their fares over. I cannot visit them where *they* are, for fear of the Glasgow uncles, Hugh and Alexander, who, after the breakup, advised me, in their own irresistible patois, of certain alterations they might visit on my face and genitalia, if ever I upset their wee sister again. In such lives, all streets are one way, and so I believed them. I abhor violence. I had one fight in my life, first year in secondary school, against a fellow who had three fingers on one hand and one on the other, and I lost. Now I'm here, on my own, in the house where I was born, in the village where I was raised, teaching in the school where I was taught. I don't do anything else. I tried keeping sheep, but gave them away, dirty bloody animals. A sheep of John Doogie's, called The Raider, breaks into my garden whenever the notion takes her, to remind me of departed joys, drops currants on the patio, squirts greenish liquid on path and pavement, then beds down all night in the doorway. Face and voice quivering, I pointed out to John Doogie that The Raider and the section of rylock fence supposed to keep her out of my garden were *his* responsibility, long agreed between our fathers and their fathers before them, and would he either secure the fence or cut The Raider's throat? He didn't deign to reply. Head half-cocked, eyes vague, mouth half-open, as if a mighty thought had struck him that only wanted uttering, he made the eldritch crackle in his throat that passes with him for mirth, then stalked off, slowly shaking his head. From the ditch from where she was planning her next move, The Raider looked up at him with brown, adoring eyes, her true earth-born companion and fellow-mortal. To stop watching television so much, and at the same time occupy my evenings profitably, I thought I might learn French properly, perhaps go back to Paris on my own next summer, or Avignon, but nothing came of it. Then I was filled with a desire to make rugs. I bought the hooks, patterned canvases, ready-cut wool, but after completing one small rug, depicting a stork at sunrise on a riverbank, for the back of the scullery door, I lost interest. Maybe this coming winter I'll take it up again. Maybe I'll get a Teach Yourself French course, even enrol in a nightclass. My wives got into the story after all. A month after the second one left, aggravated by Scandinavian furniture, pot plants and things in general, I tried to set fire to the house; fortunately for me, John Doogie appeared (God knows why), saw what I was doing and put a stop to it. So, no one ever found out; and since then I have taken control of my life, and drink isn't the problem it used to be. A colleague at the school, a divorcee, visits me sometimes, and I visit her. But I won't be getting married again. She has spoken of us living together; but after World War I and World War II, who wants to enlist for World War III?

I live as best I can, one day at a time.

I remember a garrulous buffoon from Ness, back from America and calling himself an associate professor, putting judicious fingertips together in the Social Club one Saturday afternoon and telling the assembled drouths and dungarees: *The bothans were my real university.* I remember the silence that followed this remark, the silence that prevailed as he went on, at some length, in exquisitely ordered sentences, to amplify this remark, his skull heliographing intellectual rigour underneath the bar lights whenever he nodded to emphasise the point or paused to take another sip of gin and tonic. Leaving to one side the speculation that bothans at his end of the district must therefore have promoted the public man and the acquisition of money and property as the twin greatest goods (one of his father's brothers was a minister, another was a lawyer; his grandfather on the distaff was the greatest thief that ever came out of Ness) there was, nevertheless, a germ of truth in what he said.

Bothans were small houses where the men of the village used

to meet and drink at night. Women were not allowed. Whisky and beer is what they drank, and there was a bothan in every village in Ness. For many years, because of pressure from the churches, Ness was designated a Dry Area, which meant that no one could run a properly licensed public house or hotel there, and this was how the bothans came into existence. Strange to relate, the Christians didn't object to the bothans, a case of what the eye doesn't see, or, in the village of Cross, a case of what the eye sees but chooses to ignore, as they had to soft-shoe darkly past the bothan with its thatched roof and stovepipe sticking out on their way to and from church. In our village, a small, lovely old elder, Reuben by nickname, used to come to the bothan every Saturday night, put his head round the door, say "Half past eleven, boys," and the drinkers inside, seated on benches going all round the walls, would drink up, smoor the fire in the stove, extinguish the tilley lamp and obediently troop out, locking the door behind them, in case they broke the Sabbath. That's how it was in the old days. Then, in the 1960s, the law moved against the bothans, describing them as shebeens or illegal drinking dens, and in separate court cases, men from villages at opposite ends of the district were charged with trafficking in excisable liquor. Great nonsense; but it marked the beginning of the end for the bothans. Now, in Ness, we have an inn and a social club, with fruit machines and piped music, where you can drink legally, within the stipulated hours, out of proper glasses, in clean surroundings, in the company of your wife or girlfriend if you so choose, and you don't have to go outside for a piss or a puke. We're the same as everywhere else.

Abandoning the old bothan that Reuben used to visit on behalf of the Lord every Saturday night, we built a new one at the far end of the village, away from the other houses, off the road that led out to the main road. Calor gas lighting was in this one (quicker than a tilley), an iron stove that glowed red on top, a cement floor, and plasterboard lining the walls. Seamen from the sea returning would pin postcard-sized pictures of naked orientals in interesting sexual positions on the walls, and Robert's calendar was also up there for anyone who needed to ascertain the date or the day. The gas mantle hissed, the stove glowed. Along the bench at the upper end of the house, some of the Ness football team (the famous Jonah among them), scrubbed and shining after another victory over town opposition, drank their triumphal grogs before setting out for the Friday night dance in the ATC hut in Adabrock. Jonah was going to the mainland in October, to Edinburgh university; he was going to play part-time professional football for Hibernian, he had already signed the forms. I watched him swallow a neat whisky, chased down by a swig of beer from his pint, and knew that he never would, and I was sorry.

When Kenneth came ashore for good, after his father's death, four of us took a notion to open up the bothan again on Friday and Saturday nights and go there with our carryouts. These four were myself, Kenneth, Norrie Bob and Dan from Aird. Not long after we did this, other men from the village joined in, arriving out of the night with their blue carrier bags of drink, so that the women quickly named the bothan The Blue Bag Inn. My brother John appeared several times, always on Friday nights, always with three forty ouncers of whisky and plenty to say for himself, although, of course, he never addressed me directly, nor I him. Then cars from Stornoway and the west side, heading back home from the Inn or the Social Club and seeing a light in the bothan, would turn in to the village, and meaty red faces from Bragar and Arnol, sharp-featured coves from Stornoway, cargoes of dark, silent drunkards from the fastnesses of Uig, would appear tentatively in the doorway, wondering was there anything doing and were the good times rolling again? They weren't.

This was the routine. Friday nights, after the nine o'clock news, I would collect my blue bag containing one bottle of Grouse whisky and six cans of MacEwan's export from underneath the scullery sink, implore my second wife not to wait up for me, and go down the brae to fetch Kenneth. He would be standing by the big sideboard in the livingroom the Goat's father had brought from Orkney in a zulu, waiting for me. The television would be on at a high volume, the fire banked with new peat behind an impregnable fireguard, and the old woman, Kenneth's mother, would be tightly gripping both arms of her chair in front of the television set and staring fixedly at the screen.

"Here's Donald John!" Kenneth would shout into her ear from behind.

"Who?"

"Donald *John*!"

"Hallo, Katag!"

She would look up and bare her gums at me, then immediately her eyes would swivel back to the screen.

"From up the road! Now then . . ." Prising her right hand from the arm of the chair, Kenneth would put a walking stick into it, folding her fingers over the handle ". . . Donald John and myself are going to look in somewhere and pay a visit. Keep a sharp eye on that television till Margaret [John Doogie's wife] comes to put you to bed. If anyone tries to come out of the box, show them the stick and threaten them with it. *Get back in there*, tell them, *or I'll fetch you one!* We're going now."

Outside, from the road, I could see her through the gap in the curtains: an old woman, dressed in black and far gone in the head, staring fixedly at a television set; the stick to repel boarders who have already taken over the ship clutched in her right hand.

"Now there's a symbol of Gaelic culture," I murmured.

"What?"

I looked at him.

"Oh, nothing. I was thinking out loud."

"Is it my mother?" Kenneth wanted to know. "What's a symbol?"

"Nothing. I was speaking to myself."

We walked up the brae. It was dark. The wind against us.

"I thought I was the only one who did that around here," Kenneth said. He bumped against me in the dark.

"Tinkling cymbal," he said.

In the bothan, after the walk up the road and across the inner grazings, all is warm, all is bright. I count seven, eight heads.

"Here's the scholar," Malky says.

He's drunk, or pretending to be. I put my bag with the others in the corner where Norrie Bob is. He lives nearest to the bothan and carries the key. He's in charge of the drink and the weekly sweeper and the football pools coupon.

"What kept you?" he asks Kenneth.

My face, after the night wind, burns in the heat from the stove. I sit between Panny Herroch (smell of diesel) and Allan John (hay, boiled mutton).

"So where have *you* been till this hour of the night?" Panny enquires, snuffling through his incarnadine hooter.

"Oh, don't you know, he can't bear to leave the new wife on her own at all, this man here, don't you know," Allan John booms on the other side of me.

Norrie Bob hands me a glass of whisky. I hold it up to the gas mantle. It gleams golden. There is an abrupt, tinny hiss as he opens a can of export for me. I'm where I want to be. I swallow the whisky, feeling it warm my body all the way down, dissolving all worries, irritations, responsibilities, and leaving my head clear for a good night. This is the life.

Most of the heads in here have been to sea, to war, to both. They have laboured on hydro schemes alongside Poles and Irish, done National Service, dropped into Suez by parachute. They have seen Tahiti, Chittagong, Panama, know where Trincomalee is, caught the clap in Cairns. They can make fishing flies, build houses, smell weather. They know who really shot the Red Fox. They know when the battle of Glen Shiel was, and how it fared afterwards with the Uigeachs and Spaniards. They know the story of Bonnie Prince Charlie on Scalpay, what he ate from the heel of his shoe, what he drank from a black bottle, and where the Scalpachs hid him. If she rejects the first calf, what do you do? So tell me. And now I'll tell *you*, so sit there and listen. No, *listen*, I said. They know every word and line of long local songs and poems, and of songs and poems that are not local, the whens and whys of them, how the Habost bard made his song for the first Post in Ness while with one foot he rocked a cradle, and where was the Skigersta bard when he made Dun Alasdair? Sitting with his back against a stack of barley. They know who is related to whom, and when the first Macritchies came to Ness and where they came from, and how the Port of Ness Murrays are not the same Murrays as the Dell Murrays, both branches, not by a long chalk, in fact not at all, and if you think they are you should go to that door there and let the air to your head. Sir Walter Scott met Rabbie Burns. "Is this Rabbie?" says Sir Walter. "It is, Wattie," says Rabbie. I suppose you're going to tell me now with the mouth on you that the Tailor's well on Donald John's croft is named after the tailor you had over there in Aird one time – the hump back – well, it isn't, it's for another tailor altogether, from Lionel, and before that Jura – where are *you* going? – (Malky swaying out, pretending to be drunker than he is) – is it your bedtime? – what was I saying? Jura, that's right, and he was on the run, and he was in this village first before they booted his arse out of it down to Lionel. Norrie Bob's people there are descended from him on the Lionel side of his family, the Macleans, you didn't even know your people *came* from Lionel, did you? Do you know what day it is? There's a calendar up there on the wall. Don't look at the wee jap putting it out of sight in case the back of your head starts trembling again, and before you stand up ship us another rake of drams down to this end of the waiting room. That snake never stays too long, does he? Docile and demure she looks of a Sunday evening now, boy, in her best wear coat and hat and square toed shoes, the good book held to her bosoms in a two-handed clasp as she pads the road to the Big Church, but I can remember the same one when all thoughts of salvation were far from her. What? Collie bitches in heat used to slink into the culverts against her coming.

Waal, but I donno. Give us a song, Kenneth. Go on! Do what an older and a wiser man is telling you. *O, cha b'e mo run-s' am parsail.* Give him a nip first. Do a seagull trying to swallow a herring, then. Now do Samson's dog with the sheep's head. I'll be damned. Now do a flock of starlings. Geordie trying to start the old lorry. Give him another nip. Give him the bottle. Another one of your Lionel relations is named in that song. What song? An diabhall, is that the time? What if it is? Ship us another small avalanche of drink down here, Norrie. Better not. A lot ahead of me tomorrow. Like what? Well, the sheep. What sheep? Sit on the knuckles of your arse and swallow that. One three-legged wedder and two blackface shiting at the back of the house hardly constitute a flock. Little Morag, daughter of Murdo the carpenter. Light she went she, light she went she. Go on, Kenneth! Wife of the wedding, small she. Why are you putting that light out? It's morning. So it is. Mind my head on that lintel going out. Better keep to the road all the way. Kenneth with me. My very good friend the milkman. My friend in court. He goes to the bottom of the bowl with me. Stays to the end. Going past John Doogie's, he lets out an earsplitting imitation of a cockerel. Name of God Almighty! Window going up. Margaret Doogie's voice. Very angry. I'm behind the peatstack. You bandy, red-headed blaggard! Disturbing people at this hour of the morning! But you'll rouse my John one of these days, and *he*'ll show you, just you wait, you bandy, red-headed blaggard! Window going down. Going up again. And don't think I can't see *you* crouching behind that peatstack either!

On Saturday nights, at half past eleven, as if on a signal, as if the ghost of old Reuben had once again come to the door, we would stop talking and bestir ourselves, filing out in single sober file, and leaving Norrie Bob to put out the light and lock the door behind us.

[71]

One Saturday night was different.

It was wearing on for Reuben's deadline, six of us left in the bothan drinking our last drinks, no one saying very much, when we heard the gravel outside the small window being crunched by hurrying feet. "Who in the name of . . . ?" Norrie Bob started to say, then the door opened, and framed in the sable background of night, wearing a short leather skirt, a red woollen jacket and a matching Shetland toorie and scarf, was my wife.

"Good evening, boys," she said.

She spoke in English. No one replied. We all stared at her. I wanted to be far away, in Idaho, in Basutoland. She smiled at me, and then round the bothan.

"Well, gentlemen," she said, entering and closing the door behind her. "Aren't you going to ask a lady to join you?"

Still no one spoke. She sat down daintily at the end of the bench nearest the door, next to Barlo, and crossed her long legs. She had good legs and she knew it. "How are you?" she smiled at Barlo, who was staring at her as Balaam might have stared at the ass after she spoke to him. He didn't answer.

"So this is where my man prefers to spend his weekend evenings?" she said, slowly looking round the bothan, taking it all in – the plasterboard-lined walls, the stove, the gaslight, the glasses and cans on the floor between the drinkers' legs, the bucket of rainwater in which Norrie Bob swilled the glasses; also, on this particular Saturday night, the spectacle of Allan John, in dungarees and wellingtons, stretched out and snoring on a bench at the upper end.

"I can't say I blame him, gentlemen. It's very cosy." She smiled again at Barlo, who had continued to stare at her and was now, for some reason, also nodding his head. The rest of the gentlemen were looking into their glasses, and wouldn't look up at all.

"Well?" she asked the silence. "Is no one going to offer me a drink?"

"Yus yus." Straightening up and throwing a single panicky

glance in my direction, Norrie Bob seized a nip glass from the small shelf behind him, and the whisky bottle from between his feet. "There's only . . ." He waved the bottle.

"Whisky would be lovely," she smiled. "But . . ." Her hand went to her mouth in mock dismay ". . . do you have anything to put in it? Lemonade? Water? Oh dear! Perhaps I'd better not, then." She stood up, went to the wall with the dirty postcards, studied them briefly – "Very nice!" – then spoke directly to me for the first time. "Well?" she said. "Do I have to walk the length of the dark village all by myself, Donald John darling, or will you play the gallant escort?"

I got to my feet. Only Norrie Bob and Barlo were looking at us – Norrie Bob still holding the glass and whisky bottle; Barlo still nodding his head. I wished I was in Outer Mongolia.

At the door, my wife turned and smiled sweetly.

"Goodnight, gentlemen," she said.

All the way home, she held tightly onto my arm. Now and again I had to use my torch, to make out the verge at the side of the road. She walked slowly, swaying her hips as she walked.

"You've humiliated me," I told her.

"I'm sorry."

"Made me a laughing stock. Someone who can't control his wife."

"I won't do it again."

"You're right, you won't."

"How?"

"I'm never going back there again."

"Don't be silly."

"I can't. Don't you see? You've finished all that for me."

"I'm sorry sorry sorry."

"Sure."

"Why don't you get angry? Why, for once in your life, don't you get angry?"

I didn't say anything.

"How else was I going to find out what the inside of a bothan looked like?" She tugged at my arm.

"You did that all right."

"Listen!" We were in the house and she was handing me what she called a nightcap. "You mustn't stop going to the bothan because of me. I *am* sorry, honestly." She knelt at my feet, put her hand on my thigh, looked intently up into my face. Her face, usually severe in repose, was soft and glowing. "It was a silly thing to do. I know that now. Say you forgive me. Pleeeease?"

"It's OK."

"I don't know *what* I was thinking." She moved her hand on my thigh. "Promise me you'll go back to the bothan. I'll feel bad if you don't."

"They'll have a field day with me."

"They won't."

"You don't know them. They'll never let up."

"Of course they will."

"They'll call me Donald John darling behind my back."

"I feel awful." She didn't look it. Speaking in a little-girl voice, she said, "I'm going to be very nice to you tonight, and from now on. And next Friday I'll buy a carry-out for you, yes I will, it's the least I can do, and you'll go and drink it in the bothan with odd Kenneth and the creature with the large head and the rest of your friends. Now come to bed."

And she did, indeed, buy me a carry-out in Stornoway the following Friday, she was as good as her word. I went to fetch Kenneth at the usual hour and we went to the bothan, but it was unlit, so we went to Norrie Bob's house and he gave us the key, and we opened the bothan and lit the light and lit the stove and the two of us sat there drinking and pretending nothing had changed and everything was still the same, till one in the morning. Then we went home. No one else appeared. No one appeared on Saturday night either, and the following week I decided to give the bothan a miss and go to the Social Club, and Kenneth was there before me. So that was how we started going to the Social Club. Malky offered to drive us down in the blue van and fetch us back at closing time. He became our taxi. We paid him two pounds each. After he fixed two planks lengthways for seats in the back of the van, other lads from the village, going to the Inn or the Social Club, used him for a taxi as well. They gave him two pounds each. So Malky did very well out of it. The bothan still opened from time to time; on fank days, for instance, and the young lads went there with a container of beer at New Year, but not often. And there was no sweeper or football pool any more, and Norrie Bob no longer kept the key, which was now in a plastic bag under a stone on top of the lintel, where anyone could use it, who knew it was there; and the tobacco tin containing the money for Calor gas and general upkeep was given to Babs in the Post Office for safekeeping.

After the old woman died – she'd gone blind in the end, and couldn't watch television any more – Kenneth suddenly disappeared from the village. No one knew where he'd gone. I asked Margaret Doogie if he'd said anything to her – she was still going down there for an hour every morning to clean the house, although there was no need now.

"Not a word," she said. She sounded aggrieved when she said it.

"Maybe he's in England?" I said. "With his pal from Liverpool?"

"No, he isn't," she replied. "I phoned, and he isn't."

Then one afternoon I heard the loom clattering in the shed, obviously being worked by an expert, and went to have a look. Who is this but the oldest of my brother John's stepsons. (Johnina, the cavewoman, had several by different fathers before she snagged brother John – "a five calfer," John Doogie called her.) This one is called Hector. He's pedalling away. I motion to him to stop. Kenneth had given him a contract to weave his tweeds while he was away, he replied, in answer to my question.

"Where's he gone? Did he tell you?"

"Naw."

"When's he coming back?"

"Dawnaw."

So that was that. It was the postman, a fat man who once succeeded in choking a prize heifer with the stump of a swede turnip, who gave me my first clue.

"I know where he's gone all right," he said. "But I'm no' telling *you*."

"Where's he gone, then?" I was holding the glass and the bottle. I started pouring. The whisky rose in the glass. I stopped.

"Italy," he said.

He sat down, oilskins crackling, on one of the Scandinavian chairs, and took a swallow of whisky.

"Postcards," he sighed expansively. "All the way from sunny Italy. Written in a woman's hand, very flowery. And two letters." He swallowed the rest of the whisky and stood up.

"I haven't got all day to sit here blathering to you and drinking your whisky," he said. "I work for the Crown. I don't know her first name," he said. "But it begins with 'T'."

He was gone for six weeks, and when he came back he had a woman in tow with him. She was Italian all right – the postman had been right there – but she didn't come up to any of my notions (based on films, magazines and travel brochures) of what an Italian woman should look like, being short-legged, dumpy, with close-cropped, nondescript hair, blue eyes, a shawl and ankle socks. Also, she padded rather than walked. She looked more like a woman from the west side, High Borve perhaps, possessing a knowledge of cows. But from the goofy grin on Kenneth's face as he introduced her to me, you'd think he'd won the pools.

"This is Theresa," he said.

They were going to get married. That was the announcement. I offered a drink. Theresa declined.

"I don't drink alcohol," she said.

"Theresa doesn't drink at all," Kenneth added.

"It's bad for you," Theresa said.

And how had they met?

"He wrote to me," Theresa said.

She'd put an advertisement in the *Stornoway Gazette*, looking for a Gaelic pen pal, and Kenneth had replied.

Gaelic?

"Theresa's learning Gaelic," said Kenneth.

"Is mise Theresa," Theresa said. "Tha mi gu math, tapaidh leat."

"William's going to be best man," Kenneth said.

"Your brother," Theresa said. "He's a lovely man."

William?

"He's a sea captain," she said.

I offered another drink. I thought perhaps we needed one.

"Tch tch tch," Theresa went, as she watched me pouring them out.

It turned out that Theresa didn't eat meat either. Or fish. Or chicken. Or eggs.

"They're bad for you."

She ate pasta. Fruit. Things that were good for you.

I must come down to the house for one of her pasta dishes. Lasagne with vegetables.

"It's good," Kenneth confirmed shyly. "The best of grub."

"Math," said Theresa, "agus math dhut."

They were married in the Registry office in Stornoway, and William, not in sea captain's uniform in spite of Theresa's entreaties, was indeed best man, and the captain's lady, Katie Bell, in a gown later described to me as burnt orange, Theresa's matron-of-honour. I wasn't at the wedding, but I was at the house-wedding afterwards, as was everyone in the village that could stir with the aid of a stick (except John Doogie). What a night that was! I can't remember going home! I remember that the groom and bride both sang; Theresa in Italian. Wife of the wedding, small she. "It won't be long before you're giving us *Lift on me my Pipes* in Gaelic, Teenag," I heard the postman telling her. The newlyweds went away somewhere next day; and not long after they came back, I was present at a high-level conversation in Kenneth's kitchen with Theresa and my own buxom divorcee, who happened to be over for the weekend, whose first name was Anna, and who was down with me in Kenneth's house in order to present the newlyweds with a wedding gift, a plate for hanging on the wall.

The conversation was about sex.

"What are words in Gaelic for sex?" Theresa wanted to know, sounding very voluble and Italian. She tapped me on the back of the hand. "You tell me."

I looked at Anna, whose face had assumed that happy smirk of anticipation, common to all women, whenever the talk gets dirty and could get dirtier.

"In English is cog, preeg, etcetera. You gnaw? Caant, teets, boobs . . ."

"Well . . ." I cleared my throat.

"Faag, ride, get your hole. So what do you say in Gaelic?"

Beside me, Anna made a small, squealing noise.

"No, I mast *laarn* . . ." Theresa's voice rose, she agitated the shawl with the crooks of her arms. "Tell me bed talk. What you say in bed." She tapped the back of my hand again.

"Go on." Anna nodded encouragingly at me. "You're the man with the words."

"Well . . ."

"You tell me," she said to Anna.

"Where's Kenneth?" I asked.

"They don' talk," she told Anna. "Kenneth, he don' talk. Paff paff, ow ow. In the loomshed," she told me.

On my way out, I heard her saying:

"They don' like you to go on top either. You gnaw?"

One day a year later I'm in Stornoway, outside the Broad Bay fish shop, in the company of Margaret Doogie and another woman from the village, Nellie, who's simple. Nellie has been to the optician, but is refusing to wear the glasses prescribed for her, and Margaret Doogie is trying to persuade her to put them on. Malky's big blue van turned into the Square across the road, and Theresa came out. She saw us and waved.

"There she is!" said Margaret Doogie. "The face that defies shame!"

"What face?" said Nellie, peering about. "Where?"

"Put them on, I told you," Margaret Doogie told her.

"How do you mean?" I asked Margaret Doogie.

"God pity us!" she exclaimed, so loudly that a woman going past with a strimmer over one shoulder turned and looked at her. "Are *you* blind too?"

"Who are you talking about?" Nellie wanted to know.

"Who do you think?" said Margaret Doogie. "Mistress Malky."

"Where?" said Nellie.

"Why are you calling her that?" I asked Margaret Doogie.

"Because that's what she is."

Once, in primary school, I stopped a heavy leather football, propelled from the toe of the tackety boot of Biffo John Dan (stopper centre half) with my stomach. The sensation of having all the breath knocked out of my body was not one I had ever been anxious to repeat. I was experiencing it now. I leaned my back against the wall of the fish shop. My legs were gone. Ignoring the murderous, air-polluting traffic, roaring only feet away from them, pedestrians went up and down, going about their business.

"You didn't know?" said Margaret Doogie. "Of course not. Men know nothing, see nothing. Stop that!" she told Nellie, who had put a hand with a knitted glove on it into her mouth.

"You mean . . . ?"

"Since Kenneth started working in Arnish it's been going on, don't you worry. They've run him over to his work just now, he's on the afternoon shift, same as my John, but do you think they'll now drive straight home? No fear!"

I shook my head at her.

"Instead of turning down to Ness, where do you think the van goes? I'll tell you. Straight on into Barvas, as far as the sands. Stops there for an hour. What for? To watch the seabirds? Stop that!" she said to Nellie.

"I don't believe it."

"Not that they need to be making a public display of themselves there or anywhere else, haven't they two houses? If Malky isn't in the back door of Taigh a' Ghlinne the minute Kenneth's out the front, she's trotting her bitch's tail out the docken path to him." She looked at me. "You didn't know?"

"No."

"You're the only one in the village, then. Yourself and the poor fool that's married to her."

All the way home on the bus, I brooded on what Margaret Doogie had told me; and once inside the house, I took my Zeiss binoculars from the top shelf of the Welsh dresser and placed them on the sill of the scullery window, convenient to where I'd be using them. There was no light in Kenneth's house, no van outside Malky's. I made myself a piece with butter and red jam and a pot of tea – I didn't have time to make a proper meal – and ate and drank at the scullery table. Then I put off the scullery light and sat in the dark and waited. Once or twice I wondered what I'd say if the outside door were to suddenly burst open, and my sister or Margaret Doogie appear and find me like this. "I'm resting my eyes," I would say. It wouldn't happen. The livingroom light was on. And my sister always phoned before she came down from Melbost. "I'm watching the stars," I would say. "Dammit, can't a man even watch the *stars* without ... without ... ?" It was nine o'clock before I saw the red tail lights of Malky's van stopping outside Kenneth's house. The lights went on in the kitchen, and the van drove off. I watched Theresa dump plastic bags of groceries on the kitchen table, and go through to the livingroom. The lights went on in the livingroom. Then one by one the lights went on upstairs. Suddenly the house was ablaze with lights. She came back into the livingroom – she'd changed into jeans and a sweater – went into the kitchen again and started emptying the plastic bags, putting things away into the fridge and cupboards. And just then, my eyes opened, and I knew everything Margaret Doogie had said to me was true. I watched her fill the electric kettle, put pans on the cooker. Kenneth would be home after eleven o'clock. She'd be making him something for his supper. I watched her make herself a cup of coffee, spoon sugar into it. She didn't take milk. I watched her stir something into one of the pots and taking sips of coffee. It was all true. You bitch, I thought. Two days before, when I was trying to scythe last year's grass at the back of the house, a voice behind me shouted "Eggs!" in Gaelic, and there she was, on the path, holding up a white paper poke and heading for the front door. By the time I'd managed to hurry round, she was in the livingroom, reading a short story I'd written in English and which I'd left lying on the table. "No no no no no no!" she said, when I tried to take the pages from her. I went and sat in the kitchen, resisting an urge to hurl the white paper poke against the wall. She came through. "Hay-ay," she said, and tapped me on the back of the hand. "You write the same way you . . ." She swung her arms in front of her body. "You gnaw? Scything the grass too neatly." I watched her rinse the coffee cup under the tap and place it upside down on the draining board. You bitch, I thought. You dirty, insolent Italian bitch.

Up in the livingroom, I tried to read the newspaper – I never watch television unless there's a football match on, I prefer the radio – but it was no use. I couldn't concentrate. Then I sat thinking. Before allowing him to leave the house on his wedding day, my brother William (best man) checked that the bridegroom's bow tie was straight, adjusted the flower in his buttonhole; then, preceded by a fellow walking backwards with a video camera, they came down the path together, smiling. Just after eleven, as usual, I heard the van with the back shift from the Arnish Oil Fabrication yard stopping outside John Doogie's gate, then carrying on down the brae to Kenneth's house, and resisted the urge to go through to the scullery and pick up the binoculars. A lot of Nessmen were working in Arnish. It was a big contract. John Doogie was there as a foreman. Kenneth was a rigger. Hector, my brother John's stepson, was weaving all his tweeds for him. They were earning big money, the lads in Arnish. Kenneth cleared more in a fortnight than I did in a month, and I'd been a teacher and professional man for over twenty years. I went down to the scullery, but didn't switch on the lights. He was at the head of the table, in his blue thermal working jacket with the red collar, eating supper. The goofy grin was on his face. Another fool who thinks he's happy. Mary was standing over him. I mean Theresa. Mary was the name of my first wife. She was standing over him, picking bits off his plate and shoving them into his mouth. Both of them seemed to think this was great fun. They were laughing. His oil rig cap was on her head. Then she sat on his knee and put her arm around his neck. Carefully placing the binoculars on the sill, I locked the front door, switched off the livingroom lights and went to bed.

Every night for the next week, I kept watch on the comings and goings down the brae, from my position at the scullery window. I saw plenty.

I mentioned it to the divorcee.

"It's not your business," she said, when I had finished speaking.

"No?"

"Why don't you stay over here for the weekend?" She looked narrowly at me. "It really *isn't* your business, you know."

On Saturday night, I heard the back shift van, as usual, stopping outside John Doogie's gate, as usual. I was watching *Sportscene*. I switched over to BBC 2. A foreign film was on, with subtitles. I couldn't make out the subtitles, and so couldn't follow the plot, but a blonde Amazon with bare tits was mightily to the fore. Then I must have fallen asleep. When I opened my eyes, Kenneth was grinning down at me. He had the blue thermal jacket with the red collar on, and a bottle of whisky in his hand.

"Sleeping beauty," he said.

I sat up and looked at the clock. It was two in the morning.

"Theresa's asleep. I thought I'd come and help you break the Sabbath. Here!"

He handed me a glass of whisky.

We started drinking. After getting the first one down, I livened up.

"Remember your mother?" I said to Kenneth. "Remember all the old ones that used to be in this village? They knew things we didn't. They had knowledge and wisdom."

"And indigestion," said Kenneth.

"You can laugh," I said. "But they had things we'll never have."

"Shingles," said Kenneth. "Piles."

I fetched another bottle from the bottom of the sideboard.

"I can drink this stuff like water," I boasted. "Sing *A ribhinn dhonn gur trom tha mi*."

We went outside for a piss. I showed him where I'd stuck the willow wands in the ground. "That's going to be tall trees," I told him.

"What kind of tall trees?"

"Willows."

Towards morning, I said to him:

"Listen, Kenneth," I said. "Someone's got to tell you."

He nodded placidly at me.

"About your wife and Malky. And it might as well be me."

"What about Theresa and Malky?" A frightened look had come on his face.

"Don't you know?" He made a thin, moaning noise in his

throat, but I carried on, "They're at it. All the time. Ask anyone."

"You're a liar," he moaned.

"Your house. Both houses. The big van."

"Liar." He was sitting on the couch, and had doubled over so far, his head was almost touching the floor. "Lie-ar," he moaned.

"I'm sorry." I was getting alarmed myself, the position he was in, the noise he was making. "Come on, Kenneth," I said. "Here!" I tried to shove the whisky glass under his nose. He smacked my hand away. The glass went on its side, on the carpet. He sat up and then stood up, making the thin, moaning noise in his throat and darting bewildered glances about him, as though he didn't recognise where he was. Not once did he look me in the face. "You!" he suddenly shouted, stammering and not looking at me. "*You* have to tell me! Just because you think everyone else's wife is like your own! Just because *your* wife and him . . ." He didn't complete the sentence. He reeled out of the livingroom, colliding with one of the Scandinavian chairs on his way out, and making another crashing noise in the kitchen before he pulled open the front door. I sat where I was. What had I done? What had I done? A wave of blood flooded my brain and roared back down into my face. I thought I was going to faint. I heard his feet scraping and staggering on the path, and the clang of the gate. I couldn't move. When at last I made it to the scullery and the windowsill of my undoing, Kenneth was halfway down the brae, on his way home. I have seen drunkards acquainting themselves with the corners of buildings, infants taking their first steps; but never, in my life, drunk or sober, have I seen anyone walking like that. He wasn't keeping to the road but zigzagging onto the verges and the banked grassy inclines below the verges; from my gate to where he was, in the dawn light, I could see the bright slides made by his feet in the dew on both sides of the road. Giving at the knees, he staggered to the bottom of the incline, halted, flailing his arms as though rehearsing a speech, took two or three short steps backwards but somehow, miraculously, kept his balance, before stamping unsteadily back up the bank and floundering across the road towards the verge and incline on the other side. Halted again, he turned round and contemplated the house he'd come from, causing me to back away from the window. But he wasn't looking at me. He wasn't looking at anything. I stayed away from the window after that. I didn't want to see any more. Why hadn't I stayed in Stornoway over the weekend? Why had I opened my mouth? I locked and double-locked the front door, and picked up the Scandinavian chair from its side, where it had fallen. But that was all the tidying up I did. The rest of the house I left as it was. Something else was bothering me, but I didn't want to think about it. Taking the whisky bottle with me, I went to bed.

Three times in the course of that Sunday, I was started from fitful, sweaty half-slumber by alarms below – the first time by the telephone, which I had forgotten to disconnect, ringing in the livingroom, stopping and then ringing again, until I managed to creep downstairs and pull the cable out of the wall; then, twice, by a sustained battery of fists against the front door, and a voice shouting at me to open up. The voice was Theresa's. Guts dissolving, teeth chattering, and shaking in every limb, I crouched under the downy, hiding. *Oh boys!* I kept repeating to myself. *Oh boys! Oh boys!* The whole village must have heard her. Night had fallen before I ventured downstairs again. Not daring to put the light on, I rummaged in the sideboard for the remains of a bottle of filthy cherry brandy left over from the New Year, then crawled across the carpet, reinserted the telephone cable in the wall, and after God knows how many attempts, managed to dial Anna's number in the half-light from the window.

"It's me," I said, as soon as she picked up the receiver.

"I'll get Mam," the sarcastic voice of her daughter replied. A clunk, feet going away. Silence. Feet coming. Anna's voice:

"Hallo."

"Come and get me."

"What's wrong?"

"Just come."

"You've done it, haven't you?"

"Please, Anna. I'll unlock the door once I hear the car."

"For heaven's *sake!*" she said, and put the receiver down.

Troubles, like sorrows, come not single spies but in battalions. On Monday morning, before school, I phoned my sister in Melbost and asked her to go down and feed the cat. She had a key.

"I won't," she snapped, but I knew she would, she's soft on animals.

"You can tidy the house while you're down there," I told her. I knew she'd do that, too. We're obsessive about tidiness in our family. A calendar hung crooked on the wall causes my brother William physical pain.

On Wednesday, Anna threw me out. "I want you to leave," she told me. "Now." I won't go into the reasons. Referring to her all the time as the divorcee was one. Referring to her daughter as Little Lady Nevershit was another. She drove me over to Ness.

"Are you coming in?" I asked her.

"Go to hell!" she replied.

Thursday and Friday came and went. Nothing moving, nothing doing. No one came near. I relaxed somewhat. They've calmed down, I thought. This thought consoled me until seven o'clock on Saturday night when, the tea over, the dishes washed and dried and put away, the fire banked and blazing, the phone disconnected, the television on and me in my soft chair in my carpet slippers watching it, I heard the front door opening and closing, the tramp of more than one pair of feet through the scullery, and into the livingroom came Malky, followed by Theresa.

"Hello!" I said, and made to get up.

"The man with the mouth," said Malky, pushing me flathanded back into the chair and hitting me full out on the side of the head with his right fist, and as my head went over from the force of the blow, just as hard on the other side with his left. I sat stunned. A noise in my head like a radio between stations. I could hear the television. Malky was back at the door with Theresa. I could see them clearly, even though my glasses had come off.

"... is *enaff*," she was saying to him.

"......" Malky said.

"No no no no no!" Theresa shook her head. Malky came over and hit me straight in the mouth. I sat there. He went back to the door. Theresa had my binoculars in her hand. Holding them by the strap. She was telling Malky to come away. Malcolm, she called him. They went out. I opened and closed my mouth, testing my jaw. Blood ran down my chin. Better than swallowing it. I sat there. The tuner on the radio inside my head had moved to a football match. The front door banged. He couldn't knock me out, though, the jowly, meat-faced bastard. My head seemed to be expanding. The crowd roared.

After a while, I went to have a look at my face in the scullery mirror. Glazed eyes, a bloodied chin, and a head half the size again on one side, stared back at me. I ran some water from the hot tap into a cup and rinsed out my mouth. My lips and chin were sticky with blood. The front of my pullover was also soaked with blood, so I took it off and put it to soak in cold water in a plastic bucket under the sink. Then I took my shirt off and washed my face carefully with warm water and carbolic, and put the shirt and the towel I'd used to dry my face into the plastic bin for washing. I was preparing to spray the sink and surrounds with Jif when a shiver like electricity went through me – What was I doing? Why was I doing this? – and I put the blue J-cloth back in its place on the draining board and took off the yellow rubber gloves. My head was aching badly. The front door was unlocked. It didn't matter. Let them come if they're coming. What could they do but kill me? Fumbling in the wall unit cupboard for the plastic medicine box with the aspirins, a tin of Ambrosia

Creamed Rice fell on my head. That was all right, too. Let the cupboard come down after it. Why not? Let the ceiling come down, the walls collapse. I didn't care anymore. The sky had fallen.

Maybe he couldn't knock me out, but Malky managed to loosen four front teeth for me and dislocate my jaw on one side. The teeth were removed by a dentist, and then I had to go into hospital, a great humiliation, and people in white coats with smiles and confident voices did various things to me. Lying fully dressed on top of the bed in my room on the third morning, watching a fool with a wire trolley careering round a supermarket on television and waiting for my brother William to come and collect me, my sister from Melbost appeared first, with the news that Kenneth had received a beating from Malky as well, not as drastic as mine but bad enough, and that Theresa had moved bag and baggage into Malky's house. And was I happy now?

"Someone had to tell him," I maintained sullenly, speaking with difficulty out of one side of my mouth. "I did him a favour. He'd have found out for himself sooner or later anyway."

"Oh?" she said. "Do you think so?"

"Don't try to speak," William said to me when he appeared. "I'm parked at the main door. Where's your bag?" Katie Ann was in the car. I sat in the back seat with my sister and plastic bags of groceries from the Co-op. That same day, after dropping me at my house, brother William and his wife Katie Ann went to Malky's house. They were there for an hour; but what happened and what was said in that hour will never be known by me. I know they went to Kenneth's house after Malky's, and that Malky and Theresa left the village and the island not the next day but the day after, which was the earliest booking they could get for the big van on the Ullapool ferry. William then came to my house, on his own.

"Don't speak," he said. "Give your jawbone a chance. What I have to say to you won't take long."

When he'd finished, I lowered my head, took a suck of the vitamin drink through the straw and thought: Brother, skipper, Christian, this is one man I don't want to cross. Then I looked up and looked him straight in the eye.

"Fuck off," I said.

I haven't been back at the school, I'm officially off sick, which suits my Head of Department fine: he came to see me, full of false commiserations (his father, when he was doing his National Service, got out of going to Korea by pulling faces at the officers, pretending to be mad) and told me to take all the time off I needed. So I'm here, day and night, between the livingroom and the scullery windows. I haven't my binoculars any more, I found them in the culvert beside the gate, smashed; my good Zeiss binoculars. But I go for a walk every day, hail or shine, which is why I was so glad that Kenneth came out today, at long last; you need fresh air. I thought Anna might have telephoned, to ask how I was. But she hasn't. I tried to phone her one night, late, but got the sarcastic daughter on the other end of the line. So I hung up.

We won't be like this forever, Kenneth and myself. We're good friends. We're neighbours. Women come and go. It's only a matter of time. Now that he's made a move outside, it's only a matter of time before he's turning in at my gate again. I know it. "Come in, stranger," I'll say. "Make yourself in the house and call the cat a bastard." We'll have a glass together, then, my friend Kenneth and I, and I'll never mention what he said that night about my second wife and Malky, it was the rage that made him say it, I know she had her ways but she wasn't like that. I'd have known if anything like that was going on. So mention of that will never be made by me, and we'll sit in my house and put it all behind us, and we'll be the same as we were before any of this happened. "Give us a song, Kenneth," I'll say.

[89]

What the cause of death was, we don't know yet. I saw him myself at five o'clock and he was going great guns. He'd just come back from Stornoway with a load of supplies, and a smell of drink that would have knocked over a Clydesdale. "I nearly ran over a sheep in Melbost," he shouted. "It was touch and go." And off into the house without even taking the keys out of the van.

An hour after that, Calum Dan on his way to the mill hears the dog barking and the house still dark. In he goes. He can't see anything at first. Then he sees a pair of legs sticking out at the head of the table. He switched the light on and there he was. He was on his face. His eyes open. And a cut on his forehead above one eye, where his head must have connected with the edge of the table on the way down. But he wouldn't have felt a thing. He'd switched the wireless on for the six o'clock news, as usual; the cigarette, as he'd lit it, a burnt-out streak of brown on the mantelpiece. A big frying pan of chops on the range. Calum Dan let out the dog. Then he ran to fetch his father, as fast as his legs could carry him. Together they lifted the corpse, and tidied up before the doctor.

Sisters

An afternoon in September, and two small, plump women, round-kneed and round-faced, known the country round as "The Wagons" because of their swaying galleon walk (the name bestowed on them by an old bachelor uncle) are on a bench in their sister's kitchen, a sleeping cat on a cushion between them. The sister whose kitchen they are in – Jessie – is tall as a telegraph pole and thin as a poker.

"Are you going to make us a cup of tea, now we're here?" Margaret, the eldest, asked.

"After," said Jessie.

Jessie was the middle sister, married to a man from the next village who never did a hand's turn. The Wagons were spinsters.

They were in Jessie's kitchen waiting for her son Murdoch to come and record their voices. The tape recorder, a bulky square object (property of the University of Edinburgh) was on the table, the top removed and spools in place, plugged in and ready to go.

"So where is he?" Marion, the youngest, asked.

"Where do you think?" Jessie replied. "Where is he ever?"

As if in answer, a furious ejaculation of water sounded through the cavity wall of the kitchen, followed by the high whine of a cistern refilling itself. Marion and Jessie looked at the wall. Margaret sighed.

Jessie got up and banged with her clenched fist on the cavity wall.

"Come out of that lavvy!" she shouted. "Keeping people in here waiting! A livelong day sitting on a pot!" she told the others. "Smoking ticklers and tearing at my good toilet roll. Come out of it, I said!" she banged again. "And give the air freshener a good shake after you when you do!"

She sat down again on a wooden chair at one end of the kitchen table. Pale, criss-crossing beams of sunlight sidled in through the small box window behind her. Margaret and Marion were facing the window. The sunlight gleamed in their eyes, but wasn't strong enough to make them shift from the bench. Against the gable wall, a Rayburn stove, stoked with small black peat and open at the front, blazed brightly; the lids of a large brown and a smaller green kettle on the backplate clattered in a quivering haze of heat; their spouts blew grey steam. Hunkered on a triangle of slatted wooden battens above the stove, in the corner nearest the bench, an unlagged copper boiler, sprouting a tangle of thin pipes at the top and studded down one side with rivets, churned and rumbled.

"Is it just me," Margaret sighed, "or is it close in here?" She eyed the boiler warily. "How can anyone spend their days in the same house as that contraption?" she asked. "I'd be afraid for my life."

"Look at her face with the heat!" said Marion. "Take that cardigan off!"

"It's not the heat," said Margaret. "It's pressure." She burped abruptly and then hiccupped. "Our granny's clock," she said, looking up at the mantelpiece, where, flanked by a pair of yellow china dogs (the one on the right minus one of its glass bead eyes) a clock with a front of elaborately carved wood, a stained orange dial, roman numerals, fretted brass hands and a glass door that refused to shut, wheezed importantly. "That she brought with her from Uig when she married my grandfather. Why she wanted *you* to have it, I'll never know. She used to put you in the creel."

Through the cavity wall, the lavatory sounded again.

"I'll murder him," said Jessie. "I know it. One of these days, and that day not distant, I'll have family blood on my hands."

"Stop that talk," said Marion. "Is this the machine?"

"I'm sick of the sight of it," said Jessie, "taking up space in here. Of course you haven't seen it till now. Come and feel the weight of it," she urged Marion. "You need both hands to lift it."

"I wouldn't touch it," said Margaret.

"Why?" Jessie asked her.

Margaret shook her head.

"She's put her good clothes on, did you notice?" Marion said to Jessie. "Dressed herself in the middle of the afternoon to come and talk into a machine."

"So did you," said Margaret.

"And her best shoes. We had to keep to the road all the way up here."

A sheep baa'ed loudly outside. Underneath the table, the old dog – Scot – snuffled at the noise; his forepaws scrabbled feebly on the linoleum.

"Fed up with those sheep mooching day and night around the house," Jessie said, bending to look out of the window.

Murdoch came in.

"What's the matter with your bowels, boy?" she asked him, sitting up and squaring her shoulders. "How many times have you been on that pot today?"

"Are you all *warm* enough in here?" Murdoch asked in a loud, hearty voice, crooking his arms and then swinging them above his head, like a singer inviting the audience to join in. Marion frowned at him.

"Talking of pots," Margaret rose slowly to her feet, "is it safe for another human soul to go in there after you?"

"Why is she all dressed up?" Murdoch whispered, as soon as he heard the bathroom door closing. He turned from Marion to his mother, eyes wide in anticipation, mouth open, arms crooked again. It was his way. Other times, he wouldn't say a word; wouldn't open his mouth, if anyone spoke to him.

"Never you mind about that," Jessie told him. "Is the machine ready?"

"It's all set." He touched the switch, already down, beside the plug in the wall.

"A fine autumn day outside, corn crying out to be stacked, and we're stuck in here waiting on *you*."

The lavatory flushed. Margaret came back in. "My granny's clock," she sighed. "That never lost a second." Halting a short distance from the table, she stood looking at the tape recorder. "What's that green strip of light?" she asked Murdoch.

"The volume."

"It's moving," she said. "Marion, come over here till you see this green light."

"No, but you come away from there and sit down," Marion told her. "Jessie's going to speak first."

"No I'm not," said Jessie. "Why am *I* first?"

"Who else?" said Marion. "You're the mother."

"The mother-in-law," said Murdoch.

He grinned at the aunties.

"The granny!" he exclaimed, and laughed.

"I'm always first," Jessie complained. "Why am I always first?"

Murdoch stood at the tape recorder, index fingers poised over two separate buttons. He pressed down on them. "It'll start recording," he told Jessie, "as soon as I lift my fingers. Ready?" He nodded at her once. The spools of tape whirred softly, turning.

"It's on," Margaret whispered to Marion.

"Well?" Murdoch asked Jessie. "Are you going to *say* anything?"

"I'm not ready." She shook her head. "Put it off."

"What's the matter?"

"I just said. I just told you. Put it off."

Murdoch stopped the tape recorder. He pressed the rewind button. The spools whirred rapidly backwards. "What now?" he asked.

"I wasn't ready." She stared defiantly at him. Murdoch waited, pressed down on the buttons. She nodded. He let them go. The spools started turning.

"Alan, this is your mother . . ." she began in a slow, careful voice. Murdoch stopped the tape recorder.

"Why are you speaking like *that*?" he asked her.

"Like what? What do you mean?"

"That's better."

He lifted his finger from the pause button.

"What do you mean, that's better? I'm speaking the way I always speak."

"Speak louder." He was watching the green strip.

"I will not! What do you mean, speak louder? I can't speak louder."

"Yes you can."

"I've a pain in the back of my neck. Why are *you* speaking? I thought *I* was the one doing the speaking. Alan!" she suddenly shouted at the tape recorder, "I'm sending you a piece of meat from one of Dodo's wedders next door, it should be fine in a pan of broth on Sunday, a turnip and two or three carrots planted and grown here in our own garden. I suggested a cabbage as well, separate in a plastic bag, but he said no, too much to carry already, he said, with the tape recorder and everything. What'll I say now?"

"The guga," said Murdoch.

"The guga!" she shouted. "I'm also sending you a guga, don't know the English for it, Cathy . . ."

"Young gannet," said Murdoch.

". . . young gannet, ceann a' chac beside me is saying, and I'm sorely deceived if you'll eat a gannet, Cathy, young or not. I know I can't, but here's what you do with it. Wash it first in cold water and washing soda crystals and a scrubbing brush to get the grease and salt off it, then boil it in nice clean water, then after the first boiling, strain it; it'll still be too salty, so put fresh boiling water on it from the kettle, then let it boil away to its heart's content. You'll know when it's ready if you stick a fork in it. Hang on now till I get my glasses."

Murdoch put his finger on the pause button.

[95]

"Where are they?" She'd taken a page, torn from a ring notebook and folded over twice, from her overall pocket.

"Behind you," said Marion.

"Where?" Jessie twisted the upper half of her body around in the chair.

"In the window," said Murdoch. "On top of the *People's Friend*."

"Bloody glasses." She put them on, placed the page from the notebook on the tabletop, smoothed it with the flat of her hand and read the first line under her breath. Her lips still moving, she nodded at Murdoch over the top of the glasses. Murdoch took his finger off the button.

"Cathy!" she shouted. "I told Alan chust now how to cook the guga. I said chust," she told the others. "I told myself I wouldn't and I did. Anyway," she shouted at the tape recorder, "I hope you're not too disappointed he lost his job, I'm sure he'll get another one soon, and a proper one this time, whoever heard of a Master of Arts working in a gasworks? To think he could have come over to Lewis with yourself and the two little girls last month instead of skulking on his own in the big city, a pity he didn't to keep the other drunken wretch in order, grinning at me chust now, I said it again . . . chust na galla! . . . but I could hear his carry-on downstairs, in and out of your room, Oh yes, yeb yeb yeb, annoying you and keeping you awake till all hours with his drunken babble, the mother of children. Tell my two little girls Granny Lewis will be out to Aberdeen very soon to see them. My grammar, Cathy, is not very good, so I think I'll switch to Gaelic. I hope you'll enjoy the guga and meat and carrots, make plenty potatoes with them, Kerr's Pink are the best, never mind if you can't eat the guga, Cathy, I could never eat it either; the sight alone was enough for me, not to mention the smell. Now Murdoch will be there with you tomorrow, don't make any fuss over him, don't let him drink, chust . . . I said it again . . . sorry, Cathy . . ."

She took off the glasses and started laughing.

"Thia gleidh mi . . ."

She sat back in the chair, laughing loudly, wiping her eyes.

"That it?" Murdoch asked her.

"What?" said Jessie, trying not to look at Margaret.

"It's still on. Anything else you want to say?"

"No! Yes! Wait! Alan!" she shouted. "Say your prayers! Don't drink while that other wretch is visiting you. Don't drink at all. Teach the little girls good things. Teach them Gaelic. Go to church on Sunday. Get the children baptised. Sorry, Cathy, I've no English, a ghraidh, can't speak English . . ." She started laughing again. "That's it," she said.

"You now," Marion said to Margaret.

"Has she come to a point?"

"Go on."

Margaret came over to the table.

"Where do you want me?" she asked Murdoch, her head to one side, right eye screwed up and left eye wide open and staring at him. (Her assessor look, the old uncle used to call it.)

"Here." Jessie stood up, trying to keep a straight face, and went over to the bench.

"Don't sit on the cat!" Margaret warned her. "What's that smell?" twitching her nose. "Is that you?" she asked Scot, who, from under the table, thumped his tail at her.

"Ready?" Murdoch had his finger on the pause button.

Margaret sat in the wooden chair and put her hands on her knees.

"Hello, Alan," she began. "This is your Aunty Margaret speaking. Do you recognise my voice? I didn't, the first time I heard myself. I thought it was someone else. But it wasn't."

She stopped, sighed and began again.

"Cathy, your wife, when she was here in July with the two lovely little girls, told us you've become a great housekeeper. No floor unswept, no ornament unpolished, she said. And little cork mats under the tea mugs to stop them making rings on the tabletop. Ow ow, I said to myself, when I heard it. Remember now and be good to the two lovely little girls. I never saw lovelier. We've got their picture in a frame on the sideboard, the dog smiles at them. Remember not to have any more family until my small namesake is five years old. So they can have all the attention till then. Well, we're missing you. Sorry you didn't come home with your wife and the two lovely little girls. But hoping it won't be long till you appear. Wish it was now, as unlike all other households in the village containing a man, we're getting no cuddies or saithes off the rocks. An everlasting laziness prevents your father from venturing forth with rod and line, and the only time your brother went he came back with two creatures of the deep – large heads and skinny yellow bodies – God alone knows what they were. The result of four hours sitting at Uisgebrith, smoking ticklers and staring out to America. We tried one of them on the cat: better not to speak of it."

She stopped.

"What's wrong?" Murdoch asked her. She gave him the assessor's look.

"Your brother," she began again, " has spent the entire summer in flannels and a tweed jacket, going round Ness with the large box I'm talking into. Working for some school or other . . ."

"The School of Scottish Studies."

". . . and paid big money to go round the district and up the west side as far as Borve and beyond, in and out of people's houses he doesn't know. So long as some old soul inside remembers a song or a drowning or the war in Africa. I'm on it, too. And your mother. When we were at the fishing. We answered everything he put on us. And not even a quarter of boiled sweets afterwards from the man in the big money. He's going away tomorrow. He doesn't have to. A fortnight yet before he's due back at the university. He could stay and help us lift the potatoes. But that thought hasn't entered his head. No, he must go to Aberdeen. So Alan can hear the tapes. Try not to fall out this time. Last time you were together, a claw hammer was fired through a window. Busy just now with the corn. A ladder fell with your mother, trying – what else? – to put a bonnet on a stack. It hit her on the back of the neck. Murdoch will give you all our news. I suppose we'll miss him. I gather from your mother you could have come home with your wife and the little girls after all. Remember and be good to them. If the notion takes you to write us a letter, Marion has new reading glasses. She looks like an owl in them. I better shut up now. Cheerio then, Alan againn fhìn. Nothing to say to Cathy in English. My English isn't very good just now. Keep doing the housework till a proper man's job comes along. Use old shirts gone at the collars and cuffs for the dusting and polishing. Be happy together. Longing to see the lovely little girls again, especially my namesake. I'm going to shut up now."

She sat with her hands on her knees, mouth open a little, staring at the tape recorder. Murdoch stopped the recorder. She pouted vaguely up at him.

"He nearly drowned you in a pickle barrel once," she said.

"Who?"

"Alan. When you were small. He said you went off with his crayons."

"Are you going to stay in that chair?"

Marion was at the table.

"What?"

"Go and sit on the bench," Marion told her. "There *is* a smell from that dog." She took a step back from the table, hands folded over her stomach, fingers laced, pushing up her bosoms. "I'm ready," she said. Her voice was calm.

"Aren't you going to sit down?" Murdoch had his fingers on the buttons. He shrugged when she didn't answer. The tapes whirred.

"Well, Alan," said Marion, enunciating each word precisely, and her head, as she spoke, jerking and twitching slightly, as if afflicted by a mild palsy, "you'll know who this is, you've heard her voice often enough before. I'm not going to say much, the other pair always had the advantage on me there ... Your Aunty Margaret started talking at six months, only no one could understand a word of her babble ... neither Gaelic nor Greek, as old Uncle Angus put it. Your mother, on the other hand, never uttered a word for the first two years of her life, and when she *did* speak, aged two years six months, it wasn't a word, it was a sentence, and it wasn't just a sentence, it was a question – *Why are you burning me?* – directed at our Uig granny, who had hung her in a creel on a chainhook above the fire in the middle of our old blackhouse for a punishment. Now I'm going to sing you a song, made by a man from this village, Seoras Dhomhnaill Sheoc, after he went to Canada, heartsick for home, and I hope you'll learn the words of it off by heart and sing them to yourself in the big city ... *Eilean mo ghaol, is caomh leam tric a bhith seinn*"

Sunlight touched her face and clothes, pale yellow shafts of September sunlight, moving, changed on her face to liquid gold. Her voice filled the room. Margaret looked at Jessie, went to say something, then sat back slowly, listening; and Murdoch drew back the hand that had been hovering above the tape recorder and sank into the chair at his end of the table, staring at Marion as if he had been seeing her for a long time, all his life, but was only now, for the first time, aware of her. Her voice, which a visiting professor of music, hearing the tapes months later in Edinburgh, would describe as truer than any opera singer's, filled the room. Pure as a waterbead, silencing all. She sang the four lines of each verse without pausing for breath. A shadow, a movement, in the passage outside the door, where an unshaven man in a collarless shirt and dungaree trousers held up by one brace, lured by the singing, appears, comes no further, stands there on stocking soles, listening. She stopped singing. The silence went on. Over the blue moor, the white bird flew. The spools of tape continued to turn. "Seoras," Margaret whispered, her voice quavering. Jessie's eyes were full of tears. Like one awakening from an uncommunicable dream, Murdoch reached over and pushed down the pause button. He stood up. "Sing another one!" he begged Marion. "What a voice! My God! I had no idea!" Marion gazed steadily at him but didn't reply. "Go on!" he urged, pleaded; one arm thrust vehemently above his head. "A hymn! Anything! For Alan! Anything!" Marion gazed steadily at him. The clock wheezed, the boiler rumbled. From the passage outside the door, silently as he had come, the man went away.

"We know why you're going to Aberdeen," Marion said.

Murdoch looked brightly at her. Marion held him in an unwavering gaze. His arm came down.

"We know what's taking you there. Do you think we don't know?"

"What's she on about?" Murdoch appealed to the other two in a loud, hearty voice. His mother wouldn't look at him.

"Very sorry," Margaret sighed.

Murdoch pushed down on the stop button. Halfway down, it made a dithering, grating noise and refused to go further. He released the pause button and pushed down again on the stop button. This time it went down easily. Jerkily, he pulled the plug out of the wall and removed the connection from the back of the tape recorder. He put the lid on the tape recorder and snapped shut the metal clips that secured it. Gathering up the plug connector cable anyhow, he lifted the tape recorder by its handle from the table and headed for the door.

"Thank God for that! Remember you promised to help me put those sheep to the bottom of the croft before nightfall!" Jessie shouted at his departing back. "Remember!"

They heard the door of the livingroom. A voice asking him to close the door. His feet coming back. They heard the door of the bathroom.

"We won't get another word out of him now till he leaves," said Jessie.

"Make some tea," Margaret told her. "I want tea."

"Fetch the pot from the scullery," Jessie said to Marion. "You're on your feet anyway."

"I will not," Marion settled herself on the wooden chair at the end of the table. "What a smell from that animal!"

"And two cream crackers," said Margaret. "What's the matter now?"

Jessie was clutching the mantelpiece with one hand.

"I stood up too quickly," she said.

"The blood's gone to her head," said Marion.

"No, it's the back of my neck," said Jessie. "Where the ladder hit me."

"Oh, *sit down!*" Frowning, Marion rose from the chair, and swayed across the kitchen like an uneven barrel coming slowly down a brae. "Which teapot?" she asked, from the doorway.

"The white one."

Marion went out.

"She never lost it," Margaret whispered.

"Didn't you know that?" said Jessie. "People try and sit near her in church just to hear her voice. You'd know that if you ever went."

The sun was going down. Only one side of the unpainted wooden V-lining inside the window now caught the light.

"Why do you suppose he's so mean?" Margaret wondered aloud. She turned to Jessie. "Who's he called Murdoch after again?"

"Some pal of his father's in the army," Jessie replied. "As if you didn't know. From Ross-shire. I had no say in it," she added sharply.

"Not even a black-striped ball," said Margaret.

"My ears are singing." Jessie tilted her head back. "I think my nose is going to bleed."

"You're always doing it," Margaret told her. "Leaping at things. Trying to bang through doors without opening them first."

She stroked the sleeping cat in her lap and sighed.

The princess came out of the car and came over to where we were. She made straight for us. She was lovely. "It's so nice to be here," she said. "I'm so glad to be here." Even though it was raining cats and dogs. She was lovely. Holding on to her hat. "It's so nice to be here," she said.

Visiting the Bard

That's a codling on the oval plate. Gaelic: bodach ruadh. A fisherman from the village caught him last night off the Butt, and he wasn't even fishing for white fish, he's on a creel boat. There he is. The brown old man. Tomorrow I'll gut him with my German knife and have him for dinner, boiled.

When I was in school in Stornoway and staying in the boys' hostel, there was a knife-carrying kid from Laxdale my age who used to terrorise us. His nickname was Hicka. He had a gang. Murdo Round was one of them, and I also recall a gangling lout called Donnie Modo, who was never without a fag in his mouth, had corrugated hair like a negro, and walked as if he were bobbing under a low doorway and his knees were connected with magnets. Hicka was the leader of the gang. Especially at weekends they used to stalk the streets of Stornoway, challenging the hostel boys to fight them. I was very afraid of Hicka. Through him, I acquired my lifelong acquaintance with sidestreets, corners, alleyways, closets, boltholes, the underneath of tables and the backs of umbrella stands at parties. Years later, when he was murdered in Glasgow, I wrote a poem for him.

IN MEMORIAM HICKA

Hicka the hard man is dead
(who asked me once,
outside D.D. Morrison's, Stornoway:
Do you want your head in your hands, cove?

Sunday afternoon.
Sunshine and seagulls.

I said no,

And was allowed to pass by,
Unscathed.)

Of stab wounds.
Outside the Arlington Bar, Glasgow.
And a man is helping the police etc etc.

I wonder,
Did *he* want his head in his hands
too,
cove?

Who did you say you were again? Norrie Zena's son? Zena
from Skigersta, old Calum Salt's daughter? I mean Cross-
Skigersta, the new road. That married the businessman from
Stornoway, one of the brothers? Secondhand clothes shop,
lemonade and penny chews. The Smittys. They were football-
ers. I bought a jacket off one of them once, the deaf one, Harris
tweed, the colour of carrots. Is that who you are? Norrie, your
father – Wee Smitty – was eligible to play for Ness in the Eilean
an Fhraoich cup, Zena being his mother, but he chose to play
for Point, as the Smitty side of the family were originally out
of some bog in Flesherin. So you're a Smitty.

I'm not supposed to drink the hard stuff any more, it doesn't
agree with me. What brand is it? That's a good one. Downed
plenty of them in my time. No, the roaring days are over for
me. I've been warned. A man with a stethoscope and a gadget
for wrapping round your arm and a syringe. I filled a specimen
bottle at his request with lime green pee. Also, he cupped my balls
and stuck his finger up my arse. But you go ahead. Glasses in that
cupboard. No, the one next to it. If Bellann hasn't shifted them
again. She comes in daily to attack the premises with cans of
spray and yellow dusters and hoovers. Keeps shifting the glasses.
You won't have one either? You don't drink whisky. You'll have
a beer, if I don't mind. Go ahead. Why should I mind? Is that
what's in the other plastic bag? I'll even have one with you. Beer
I'm allowed. It's lager. Whatever.

So, you're a student. In the university of Glasgow. Celtic studies. Well, that's no surprise, considering the brains on both sides of your family. Wasn't there a Smitty was nearly Governor General of Tasmania? And Zena's brother Malcolm wrote a short history of the Ness Morrisons, published privately, and where do you leave grand-uncle Bobo, another scholar if ever there was one. Slainte! No, don't put me on a tape recorder, I'm not keen on the sound of my own voice. Put me on but don't play me back. I'll give you one of the Shamus poems. Can you speak Gaelic, or are you a Stornoway cove and only able to understand it, like my dog? You're learning. Here's a Gaelic poem. I'll say it in English.

SHAMUS AMONG THE CREW AT THE PEATS

Not the hollow-cheeked, unshaven one
sucking a tickler,
or the one in the white seaman's cap streaked with
   red lead
talking of Fiji,
or the fat one in yellow oilskins
prophesying rain,
or the one with the spade and the frown
waiting for the tractor to bog down to the axle,
or the one from the next village, the man's wife's cousin,
who gobbled the last of the half-bottle,
or the one hunkered down apart,
crumbling a peat between his fingers . . .

. . . but the one in the tweed bonnet and bib overalls,
and wellingtons not folded at the top,
who, consulting the interior of the pan loaf piece,
shakes his head over the ubiquitous spam,
and knows where the boundary stone is,
under the long grass.

Two poems already. I'm going well tonight. Who's Shamus? Hold on two ticks, it's thirsty work remembering lines. These

cans used to have voluptuous girls in bikinis on the back of
them, back in the oats. Names like Linda and Veronica. Now
if I was a modern Gaelic poet, complete with fat dictionary
and book of wise saws, a flamboyant beard and a voice like the
Glasgow underground, I would be explaining to you, even now,
how the English version of the poem I just recited isn't a patch
on the Gaelic one, and, indeed, must not be judged as poetry
at all, impossible as it is, I would say, sipping my tonic water,
to communicate the linguistic subtleties, nuances, rhythms,
assonances, alliterative and onomatopoetic mellifluousness of
the original in English, or, indeed, any other language on earth.
Shove us over another can there. Tastes like old spinster's piss,
than which, according to my late friend Archie from Uist, there
is nothing more efficacious or soothing for cracked hands and
ragnails. It's a specific, according to Archie. Shamus? Who
knows?

SHAMUS IN THE INFANTS' CLASS PHOTOGAPH

Two boys, and Tammy's girl, have their eyes closed.
All the girls have ribbons in their hair.
Peggy Ann Macritchie is laughing.
Murdina Smith beside her was best at Arithmetic.
She became a lady missionary.
Third from the left, second row – Deena – died last
                                                    year
In Crieff.
And Alan Angus, two years before that (heart attack).
And K.D., aged nineteen (drowned in Hamburg).
Miss Murray isn't in the photograph.
She was their teacher.
She wouldn't go into photographs.

All but Shamus are facing the camera.
Second back row, aged six,
He is peering into John the Coat's ear
At the ball of cottonwool.

He can read the *Daily Express* and the *Bulletin*
And Cathy Ann Handaidh from Swainbost (absent)
Helps him with his wellingtons
At the end of the day.

Gaelic too, that one. These cans are very bracing. No, I won't
say it in the original. I know you would. I know it would be.
But I'm not saying it. Taigh na beetch air a' Ghaidhlig. You
don't smoke, by any chance? You mustn't put the tape recorder
on, I detest the sound of my own voice. I'll say "The Sheriff
of Fractured Jaw" now. A fellow in the village. How he got
the name. Is that another can you're giving me? Pop goes the
weasel. 'N diabhall, seall air a sin! I've cut myself. I'm bleeding.
But good for the thirst, lager. Especially if, like me, you put
away two slabs of salted Norwegian ling for your dinner, and
an ashetful of ragged spuds boiled in the old style with the
eyes still in them. A fag is good with a can of beer. Lager. A
cigar. But you don't smoke.

The Sheriff. Lives at the other end of the village. Awkward
wrinkled runt of a man, God knows how old, stubborn as shite
in a blanket. Forever feuding and falling out with people. I had
a photo of him on the mantelpiece once, Bellann must have
tidied it away. One of your townies, delivering a fridge next
door when he happened to be in there, nicknamed him the
animated raisin. After he left, the townie asked the woman, "Do
yous no' bury your dead in Ness?" A man that knew everything.
Family tree? Come to him. Local history? He'd put you right.
Law? Forget Colin Scott. At the same time, he kept astrology
charts, believed in the evil eye, feared Friday the thirteenth,
the cuckoo's voice too close to the house, and would turn back
if he met a minister or a black cat on the road. I don't know
why I'm talking about him in the past tense, he's still alive. I
warned him not to bother the Macdougalls. Don't bother the
Macdougalls, I told him. They're volatile. They come labelled
with skulls and crossbones. He wouldn't listen. Who listens to
a poet around here? Who listens to a poet anywhere? I am held

in the same regard in this village as the village idiot used to be, before they abolished him. Another swig first.

THE SHERIFF OF FRACTURED JAW

Telling himself
that his cause was just
that right was on his side
that a long-standing injustice had been perpetrated by
                                        one family
not only against him but against his father before him
and *his* father before *him*
that the old inaccurate croft boundary lines redrawn and realigned by a specially convened committee of Land Court surveyors confirmed the marches of his family's apportionments on the common grazings in perpetuity immune from squatters
that the maps were now accurate
that the documents were in order
that the records were unequivocal
that it was there in black and white
that the factor had the facts at his fingertips
that the councillor would back him up
that the lawyer was raring to go
that the time had come
that the season was here
that the signs were favourable
that the runes were propitious
that Mars was in Leo
that to delay for a year would be to delay forever
that he who does not sow on the cold day will not reap on the warm
that his grandmother's dream had substance
that the appearance of a wet ball of wool on the gatepost
                                        was no accident
that his maternal grandfather had uttered a true
                                        prophesy

that the neap tide had rustled her silks
that the stonechat had alighted on a bare rock
that the mare's foal had turned her arse to the wind
that Ivor's daughter was in her hole
that a beast with the head of an adder and the tail of a
peacock had been seen on the foreshore in Arnol . . .

he took pen in hand
and wrote a letter
in good hard English
to the Macdougalls, Benview Cottage,
announcing his intention to proceed against them
immediately if not sooner
with the full might and machinery of the law.

Whereupon
two days later
one of the Macdougalls
D.J.
(not the largest
or loudest
of them)
came over the rylock fence between the houses
without breaking stride
and with one punch
loosened his back teeth on one side
made him bite through his tongue
and left him on his back
in last year's potato patch
observing new constellations
in the afternoon sky.

So. Let's see, can I remember the names of the boys in your
father's family. Gook, Croppy Jimmy, Big Smitty, Whosays,
Wee Smitty and Chondo. And one girl, Lucy. Did I leave
anyone out? I think another can. You've more in the car? Open
it for me. Don't want to lop my finger off. And in grand-uncle

Bobo's family, Head-the-Ball, Satch, Charlie Comeup, Gogo
and Neilly Bob who played centre forward for the Aths.
I'll tell you something else goes well with lager. Whisky.
Neat, no water. Followed by a swig of this sgloosh. I said
no hard stuff, I know, but I'll have one. Open the bottle
with your long hands and your strong hands. Glasses in the
cupboard there. The other one. Sure I'm sure. That's good,
keep going. Wee touch more. Not having one yourself?
And I'll say my Tomintoul poem to you. I was there
at a wedding. Gaelic: Tom an t-Sabhail. Got stranded
there, dunno, week, eight days. Snowed in. Know where
Tomintoul is? Came home via Hamburg, Germany and
Eccles, Lancashire.

No, it's all right. I'm all right.
Jesus!
Phew! Wha'?
No, leave the bottle there. No no.
Have one yourself. Go ahead.
Right. Is the tape recorder on? Shove it on. Is it on?

IN TOMINTOUL

I can have a good time anywhere,
The small woman from Aberdeen said.
I don't have to heiter over the Lecht
To have a good time.

She was very small.
Red hair. Double vodkas and tonic.
The Marmoset, she was called,
But not to her face.

All roads out of Tomintoul are blocked.
There's no way out.
I'm still in my Friday night suit.
More snow is forecast.

Means *hill of the barn*, I tell her.

The Lecht?
No, Tomintoul.
That's Gaelic, is it? the barman said
(butting in).

Suppressing a shivery yawn,
I order another round.
Whisky. Large vodka and tonic.
One to yourself.

We're the second highest village in Scotland,
The barman said.
Do you know what the highest one is?
Wanlockhead.

I've the constitution of an ox,
The Marmoset continued,
Taking a heavy gold lighter from her bag
And lighting a Marlboro.
Dink went her lighter
On the glass tabletop.
I'm never sick.
Never get headaches.
What day is it?
Monday, the barman said
(butting in again).

That could be down to the quinine,
he said.

In the tonic,
he said.

More snow is forecast.
The Marmoset examines her shoes for tidemarks.
Any minute now the barman will tell me
Where Wanlockhead is . . .

There's no way out.

A Gaelic proverb just came into my head. Better a patch than a hole. Ancient wisdom of the Gael. No, leave the top off. Look at that hand. Steady as a rock, cut finger or no cut finger. Doctors? Stay away from them. Start hanging around doctors' waiting rooms, lawyers' offices, Gaelic colleges, you're done for. Teachers! Jesus! Lecturers! But then, you're already in the Gaelic world. Saoghal nan Gaidheal. You'll end up a professor. Why not? You can't speak the language. Which gives you a good headstart. A poet, then. A nua-bhard. Everyone in the Gaelic world – all these smooth commentators, leeches, salaried termites – are poets. It's a poetic language. They write about feelings. Perhaps a novel? Unbearably cute people who never were talking interminably about nothing in an idyllic landscape that never existed. Or a commissioned, quintessentially Gaelic play, wittily entertaining yet serious, which explores questions about faith and identity, the second sight, the Clearances, language and culture, the herring fishing, Presbyterianism, alcoholism, traditional song and story, the mischievous spirit present in every modern Gael and the music of the great bagpipe. No, didn't see it. Didn't see that either. Where's the bottle? Bellann got me a thing, whatdoyoucallit, plastic, putanan, to point at the telly. Remote control. I can't work it. If you've a good foundation of salt fish or sausages in your stomach, you can drink anything. Archie Uibhist told me that. Slaint'! Gaelic's done for. Is the tape on?

GALE WARNING

Close up the henhouse
Anchor the stacks.
The dog before his master
chap chap chaps.

Storm clouds gathering
In the south.
Put on the porridge pot.
Stay in the house.

Daddy's in the hospital
in a white bed.
Nil by mouth
above his head.

Watch for the blowdown.
Don't burn your tongue.
Are all the children in their beds?
Mammy has gone.

Gone down south
With the English man.
Write when you're able.
Phone when you can.

Keep up your Gaelic.
Daddy's gone south.
Mallin, Rockall, Hebrides.
Nil by mouth.

Now play it back till I hear myself. Is that me talking? In yill arams. It's been on all the time! It *is* me. There's the clock ticking away in the background. Hui ui ui! Don't put me *off*! Dog before his master? That's the small buffet of wind comes before the main blow. Called the wind chap by east coast fishermen. Chap meaning knock. As in dominoes. One of Grandpa Broon's cronies is always chapping at dominoes. First footing the Broons, what's on the Hogmanay table? Black bun and ginger cordial. And Hen in his waistcoat and Joe playing the bagpipes. Beloved of Mendelssohn, first name Felix. Shakespeare wasn't keen on the bagpipes either. Screech like parrots at a bagpiper. Others, when the bagpipes sing i' the nose, cannot contain their urine. The porridge pot? 'S math am brochan 's tac an teine. On a day of wild weather, be glad of the porridge pot and the fireside. Never heard that? Old Gaelic saying. What we'll do, once I quaff this bumper of the amber, we'll take the bottle and go and annoy the old bastard next door. Peter. Ask to put him on the tape, watch his head

wag. What we won't do is play cards with him. After that we'll
go and annoy the other old bastard next door. Murdo. He's a
believer. As sound a Presbyterian as ever popped a pandrop. I'll
put "Bilingualism" on the machine for you. Poem I wrote for
Bellann. Then we'll go to the Cross Inn for another bottle and
come back here and I'll put Gaelic songs on the contraption
for you. I've a very good singing voice. A light baritone. *Tha
mi tinn 's mi ri caoidh mo dhochais. Nochd 's a-raoir . . .* Is it
on? Day, da-di day da-di di-di di day-O. What poem? For
Bellann. Yes, and after that, in my light baritone, I'll sing
you a selection of Old Favourites from the district, *Eoropie
O Eoropie, The Brown-haired Lass of Fivepenny, Knockaird of
the Cold High Bens, Port Port soon shall I see thee O, There is
no Peat in Manitoba, Adabrock though far you're from me, The
Green Fields of Habost, The Day we killed the Brindled Cow, Dell
where as a youngster I, Dram we will nor drink with cheer while
the Bailiff is alive* and *The Great Song of Galson.* You'll need
another tape. Here's the poem.

BILINGUALISM

I can't mind my p's and q's at all
in English
f's and c's all over the place
As for the other tongue
I'm mainly a blasphemer in that one
The third commandment
takes a severe pasting
every time I open my mouth
And when godly people
or the common five eights
remonstrate with me
I resort to more bad language/blasphemy
To make them stop
Get off my back, you holy cunts!
I tell them
You common five eight (eights) cunts!

Thighearna Mhoir! I add
In the other tongue
I know it isn't poetry
It doesn't scan
Any common or garden
Christian
could tell me that
Bellann.

Brùc. Now play it back. Listen to myself. Is that me? Put me off. Bellann was in today. My niece. When are you going to take that shirt off? she said. Never, I said. That's what you think, she said. Upshot: the shirt I was wearing then is not the shirt I am wearing now. Where's the bottle? Why is there no milk in this house? she said. Milk is for babies, I said. Archie Uibhist told me that. Haraag! Your great grandmother, Barbara, was notorious in Wick at the fishing. Zena's mother. Zena herself wasn't slack in that direction either. Ask the Sheriff if you don't believe me. Man that knows everything. After another one – don't want any more of that sgloosh, full of chemicals, swells you out – go to Cross Inn. On our way back look in on the Sheriff. "The Sheriff of Fractured Jaw". I made a poem for him. Gaelic, then English. Did I? An diabhall! But your Ness great grandfather – now there was a strong man. Tormod Mor. That's Big Norman in the other tongue. A strong man. Barrel of coarse salt he took from Stornoway to Ness on his back. Haraag *craag*! I've a very good light nasal baritone. Going in for the Mod next year. The Traditional. Oldest competitor since Big Mary of the Songs had a go in Oban, back in the oats. *'S a chailin bheag dhonn, nach tarraing thu null* . . . He says to my father. Tormod Mor. Ookie, he says. For our breakfast in Fort Cheorge we got a haraag hard tack biscuit *nach tarraing thu null* you wouldn't give to a haraag mangy dog. *Nach toir thu dhomh rum.* And a cup of cold tapwater. *'S a' fuachd ann.* Them was the days, Ookie. Tormod Mor said. And marching to the sound of the bagpipes. Couldn't march the same to a brass band. Or Mendelssohn. Couldn't keep the step. Wee Donald Macleod was Pipe Major in Fort George. Had Shakespeare heard Wee Donald Macleod on the bagpipes, he'd have changed his opinion of the instrument.

> *Hai-dàlum ba dàri am*
> *A-hai dirì a dàri am*
> *Ba hai-dum ba hà-dum*
> *Ba harum hai dirì*
> *Haidil-a ba haidarum*
> *A hidir-eadar hai-dalum*
> *Hiodarum ba-hà dirì is pìob Pholachàir.*

Ta, an yill. Fuggin empty bottle. Get another. One hidden wellington boot where not here. No no no! In case Bellann. Who? I'm ok. Eeshd oos! Get other bottle. Maybe the barn. Cross Inn. Brùc. There's the ling coming up. All the way from Scandinavia. Haraag ag ag. Should I hazard a fart? That codling I bought today from the fish man. Think how big his eyes were swimming up the Atlantic. We're a fish-eating people. But bad days are upon us. When did you last clap eyes on a halibut? O thou, who, by thy hand, hath foreordained, whatsoever comes to pass, and all very good (take your partners for a boiled eel), when the cod and the ling are gone, and the gurnet and the skate are no more, and the haddock has vanished, and the flounder is a memory, and the cuddy and the saithe no longer nuzzle the seaweed in Geo na Muic, and the lythe is a picture in a natural history book, shall we then, mutton-eaters to a man, be cast out, heliogabalus, on the rollocks of our arsebones, between Cockbridge and Tomintoul, forever and ever? Alas!

Old bastard next door. Wouldn't mind giving him one, side of the noggin. He wouldn't feel it. Made of india rubber. Like the Michelin man. Noise your fist would make on him: *chunk!* I'll bet you that German knife of yours, says he. After taking all my money. Call, says I. King straight flush, says he. Bellann got my knife back. *Wheek!* he goes, from his end of the table.

Wheeeeeek! Better stand up . . . What? No no no. Do it myself, own steam. Heeshd. Who're you? See? Standing. Cannot a man stand and sup a glass of stimulants at his own fireside? Don't worry about that, Bellann'll clean it in the morning. Sit down, why? I'll bloody stand own house, 'n yill. Zena's niece nephew. Haveeng orr ma yayin. Hicka the Bastard! *Do you want your head in your hands, cove?* Tolas! That was another one. Hicka's gang. Little blond bastard. Murdo Round. Bastards! Come on, says I. Bloody bastards. You and whose army? Mise fuggin bastards Niseach broo joll. Take the lot of you on. Like that! And like that! Come on, the fuggin pack of you! Bloody bastards!

Yus yus yus. Heesh.
Quiet now.
In yill arams . . .

Ah, ta ta ta ta BUT!
'N yill arams . . .
Haraag!

An yoo? Hoo yoo, 'n yill arams?
Erchie, is it?
Hoo yoo co yoo?
Haraag ag ag . . . Hui! Weesh!
Eeesh cheeesh cheeesh cheeesh cheeesh.
Hoosays?

Ta ta ta BUT! HEEESHD!
Erchie, is it?
Erchie Ooeeeshd, 'n yill, where Erchie?
Dead gone kaput.
Cold cold ground.
Weeping. Ai . . .

Hui! Hoo yoo, 'n yill, goggling at, bass turd?
'N yill . . . HOO?

Veek in yill! Me Tolas Macs Bar bang in yill fuggin
 bass turds.
YOU WERE THERE!

Uh vass . . .
Turd.

I hauled the plank from the shore. I put it crossways on the kitchen table. I measured it.

It was thirteen feet in length, measured from both ends, two feet wide and four inches thick. Hard wood. I kept the figures in my head.

I went over to Thomas's house to borrow a saw. Thomas's wife gave me a saw.

My wife was in, when I came back from Thomas's house. She told me to take the plank out of the house. I refused.

I measured six feet and six inches from one end of the plank. I made a mark with my thumbnail.

I measured six feet and six inches from the other end of the plank. I made a mark with my thumbnail.

I made a line with a pencil between the two marks.

I started to saw the plank, keeping to the line.

My wife's face, and the face of Thomas's wife, came to the kitchen window. They went away.

I cut the plank in two halves. I measured them.

One half was six feet and six inches long, and the other half was six feet and four inches.

How could that be?

I did something wrong. But what?

Sawing through the plank, I sawed at the same time through the wing of the table.

I don't know what I did wrong.

My wife came in. She screamed when she saw the table.

If it was six feet and six inches from one end, and six feet and six inches from the other end, how is one half six feet and six inches and the other half six feet and four inches?

My wife went away to Point for a fortnight, to stay with her sister.

Where did I go wrong?

The Odour of Corruption

Although there was a death across the road from me – old Maggie Mary – I was still able to carry on tiling the new bathroom I'd installed upstairs, a noiseless, invisible activity that wouldn't offend the mourners. I'm a joiner to trade, took out my trade on the island; but a man with one trade can easily turn his hand to another ten.

I was on my own in the house. The morning after Maggie Mary's death, Norman came over. After the prayer meeting; he was still in his suit. I was on a small step-ladder, in my blue boilersuit and trainers.

"You're busy," he said.

I could smell the drink on his breath.

"Nora's coming home for the funeral," he said.

"Is she?" I came down off the step-ladder. "Want some tea?" I said.

I hadn't seen her in over twenty years.

Ahead of her arrival, he asked me to come over and help him take the heavy, framed picture of their father down from the livingroom wall and put *The Ship of Faith* in its place, to cover the clean square of wallpaper.

Nora was Norman's sister, older by two years. She was married down in England, in Hartlepool, to an airman she met at a dance in RAF Uig. The day she left home to marry the airman, her father had sent the following javelin speeding between her shoulderblades – *The door you are closing behind you will never be opened by you again* – and she'd taken him at his word, she'd never come back home, not even to his funeral. Nora didn't look like Norman, she was long and thin and dark, a face full of bones that moved whenever she spoke, and she had her father's frown and temper. The town where

Stephenson built the Rocket – that's where she is. Hartlepool
was where they hanged the monkey.

After shifting the pictures for Norman, I went back to
the tiling, but my mind wasn't on it. So I packed it in for
the day. It's no use going at a job if your mind isn't on
it.

Nora was supposed to be on the first ferry, but it was late
afternoon before I saw a large blue Volvo arrive outside their
house, and a short, fat man in a cream-coloured flannel suit
and fedora hat get out on the driver's side, and a thin woman,
who towered some twelve inches above him, on the other.
The woman went straight into the house, and Norman ambled
out and gave the short, fat man a hand with many pieces of
luggage, including a cardboard box. I waited until the house
had filled with people for the nine o'clock prayer meeting.
Then I went over.

Among cars just as large and shiny, belonging to the more
opulent Christians in the district, the blue Volvo was distinguished by the name of a Blackpool motor dealer on a sticker
in the rear window. The house was jam-packed with mourners.
I sat in the kitchen, near the door, on a wooden folding chair
from the church hall, next to an old woman, John Allan's
widow, who had a brooch containing what looked like an
oystercatcher's egg at her throat, and stank of mothballs and
lavender water. "You Satan!" she said to me. Nora, dressed in
black, moved among the crowd in the livingroom. She saw me
and came down.

"It's you," she whispered, taking my hand in both of hers.

"It's me."

"And still as full of the Satan!" John Allan's widow informed
her.

Nora's eyes, tawny brown like a cat's, glinted at me in the
light of the room, out of the boney angularity of her face. The
skin on her face was smooth, apart from the crows' feet at the
corners of her eyes. She was beautiful.

"I'll see you after the prayer meeting, don't dare leave," she whispered. "How long is it, twenty-two years?" The murmurous hum of conversation in the livingroom subsided; there was coughing and a clearing of throats. "They're starting," she whispered. "I must go."

The prayer meeting over, women and girls started serving tea. I was handed a tiny china cup on a saucer and a sideplate that wouldn't stay on my knee. "Tree sugars, a ghraidh," John Allan's widow beside me said to the girl. She champed steadily on a bun. A minister I'd never clapped eyes on before, a young man, appeared from the livingroom, showing his teeth in the beatific smile peculiar to some of his calling, and set off along the front row of chairs, shaking hands with everybody. He was flanked by two of the village elders, spiritual minders. I had fallen out with both of them. They were my mortal enemies. "How are you?" the minister kept repeating. "And you're well?" I rose to go, leaving my cup and saucer and sideplate on the chair. John Allan's widow shook her head at me. Norman followed me to the door.

"Come over later if you get the chance," I told him. "I've got a bottle."

(Although I don't drink myself, I have it in the house for visitors.)

I went back across the road then, drew the curtains, did my evening exercises (designed to relax mind and body) and had my supper of milky cocoa and two dry Cornish wafers. I was in my dressing gown and carpet slippers, watching a late nature programme on the television about the Congo, when the phone rang.

"Get over here," Nora's voice said.

"I'm in my pyjamas and slippers," I told her.

"I don't care if you're in your nightgown and slippers," she told me. "Get over here."

Outside the house of mourning, the blue Volvo was on its own again. The outside light was on, the kitchen lit up.

"Switch the lights off behind you," Nora's voice shouted from the livingroom. "We don't want anyone else tonight."

Up in the livingroom, Norman said:

"This is my brother-in-law. Geoffrey."

"Ow do," said Geoffrey.

"Geoffrey, John Murdo. Our neighbour."

"Hello, Geoffrey."

We shook hands.

"Geoffrey's a joiner as well," Norman said. "He's got his own business."

Geoffrey had taken off the cream flannel jacket, the red velvet waistcoat and the shiny silk tie that had marked him as *one-not-from-here* at the prayer meeting, and was in leather slippers. His cream flannel trousers were held up by red and yellow striped braces. From the way he stood poised at the sideboard, head tilted in enquiry and holding up an empty cut glass tumbler, he seemed to be in charge of the small squad of bottles arranged there. I saw whisky, Irish whiskey, gin. A forty-ouncer of vodka. I warmed to Geoffrey.

"Sit down," Nora said. "Geoffrey'll get you a drink."

She had changed out of her black, and was now wearing a white blouse and red skirt.

I put the bottle of Grouse and the large bottle of ginger ale I'd brought over with me on the sideboard.

"Just a ginger ale for me," I said, indicating the bottle.

"I told you," said Norman.

"You sure, lad?" said Geoffrey.

"Sure," I said.

"He's in the AAs," Norman said to Nora. "I told you that."

I warmed even more to Geoffrey when, after handing drinks to the three of us, he poured himself a half-tumblerful of the Irish whiskey, made a small noise in his throat, and in one movement swallowed it down neat.

"I think you must have Scots blood in you, Geoffrey," I told him, after watching this feat.

"Irish," said Nora.

"English," said Geoffrey. "Born and bred."

Without thinking, I sat in the old lady's chair. "Look where I've planted myself," I said, and made to get up.

"Stay where you are," said Norman. "My mother won't be needing it any more."

He laughed.

"She'd *want* you to sit there," he said.

"She was always so fond of you," Nora said. "Her letters were always full of John Murdo and what John Murdo was doing."

"Fond!" Norman exclaimed. "Fond isn't the word!"

Nora got up and went to lock the front door. She came back. "My favourite men in all the world," she said. She was drinking vodka. She took Norman's glass, and Geoffrey's, and refilled them at the sideboard.

"Here you go, boys," she said. "Let's have a proper wake." She handed me a glass of whisky. "One won't hurt you," she said.

I studied the tawny liquids in the two glasses I was holding. Nora smiled at me. "Look at you!" she said. "Look at him!" she said to the others.

"What about him?" Norman asked her.

She sat back beside Geoffrey on the couch, still smiling at me. I poured what was left of the ginger ale into the glass of whisky.

"Good luck." I swirled the liquid in the glass and took a long, steady sip. There was a silence. I looked round at their faces.

"I'll be damned," said Norman.

"Cheerio," said Geoffrey.

"Never thought I'd see the day again," Norman said.

"You all right, lad?" Geoffrey asked me.

"Fine."

"Oh, come *on!*" Nora protested. "You'd think I was trying to *poison* him!"

"I'm fine," I said.

We started talking about football. Rangers had been playing

earlier in the evening. "By the time the last of them got themselves out of here, the highlights were over on the telly," Norman complained.

"What team do you support yourself, Geoffrey?" I asked.

"Preston North End."

"I thought he was from Hartlepool?" I turned to Nora.

"*Hart*lepool?"

"I mean Blackpool."

"I'm from Preston," Geoffrey said.

"Why did you think he was from *Hart*lepool?"

"I thought you were from Blackpool," I told Geoffrey. "I'm a Preston North End supporter," I told him.

"Get on!" said Geoffrey.

"Since 1948, when England beat Scotland at Hampden. Tom Finney, Preston, was outside left for England."

"Right," said Geoffrey.

"Ian Black, Southampton, was the Scotland goalkeeper. We lost two nothing. Finney scored the first England goal."

"John Murdo's got a memory like . . ." Norman told Geoffrey.

"The Preston plumber. What was he like to watch?"

"Who, Tom?" Geoffrey screwed up his eyes. "I remember," he said slowly, "whenever he got the ball, the crowd would go silent. It were strange, that. Thousands of people going silent."

"Deepdale," I told Norman. "That's the name of Preston's ground."

"Ibrox," said Norman. He took a huge breath.

"So who was the better player?" I asked Geoffrey, after waiting in vain for Norman to say something else. "Finney or Matthews?"

"Tom were more of an all-round player," Geoffrey replied. "Two-footed. He could play right or left wing."

"Or centre forward," I said. "Against Scotland at Wembley, in 1951, with England down to ten men, Finney moved to centre forward. He scored against us that day too. But Scotland won, three two."

"Didn't I tell you!" said Norman. "Ask him who was the first man to fly."

"Stan were a right winger, pure and simple," Geoffrey said. He pronounced it wing-ger.

"That was another Englishman we couldn't handle," I told him. "In 1955 . . ."

"So who's the one from Lochs you're married to?" Nora asked me.

"Joan? She's from Laxay." I found I was still addressing Geoffrey. "They're over in Lochs just now, herself and my daughter. Visiting the granny."

"You've a daughter!" Nora said gently. "How old is she?"

"Fourteen. Going into second year after the holidays."

"I'd like to have seen her."

"She's clever," said Norman. "Watch her on the computer! My word!"

"And is she a daddy's girl?" Nora asked. "Mine are, both of them." She nudged Geoffrey with her shoulder.

"I suppose . . ." I said.

(Not so. She has what my old aunty would call a demon of contradiction in her, and finds it impossible to tell the truth about anything. Twice I've been summoned to that school in Stornoway because of complaints about what they call her attitude. The truth is she's over in Lochs to see if the granny, a former headmistress, can drum any sense into her, before it's too late. I know I can't.)

"And Crissie Hamish?" Nora asked me. "What happened there?"

I shrugged. "Who knows?"

"Were you engaged to her? Someone said you were engaged to her."

"I don't know." My glass was empty. "Yes."

"So what went wrong?"

"Her father was against it. Hamish. And her mother."

"That stopped you?"

"It stopped her."

"Belly up," said Geoffrey. He took my glass, and Norman's, and went over to the sideboard.

"It wasn't to be," I said.

"They *live* in Hartlepool!" Norman suddenly announced. I hadn't noticed till then how drunk he was. "That's why you thought Geoffrey was from . . . from . . ."

"Darlington," said Nora.

"Here you go, Norman." Geoffrey was back.

"A fellow from the Highlands played for Preston the same time as Tom Finney," I reminded Geoffrey. "Tall, thin, dark fellow. Angus Morrison."

"Left wing-ger," said Geoffrey.

"Tall, thin, dark fellow," I said.

"Why wouldn't you go to Spain on the free holiday?" Nora asked me. Norman stirred in his chair, then sat back, laughing, right leg raised, and holding his right knee between interlocking fingers. "John Murdo won a free holiday to Spain," she told Geoffrey. "In a magazine competition. A fortnight. He wouldn't go."

"Who told *you*?"

"Not guilty," said Norman, laughing and shifting about in his chair. He must have been tippling at it on the quiet all day.

"I didn't want to," I told Nora. "I've seen young ones here at that carry-on, saving for fifty weeks of the year to spend a fortnight in Spain. Coming back riddled with fleas and diarrhoea."

Geoffrey was tinkling behind me at the sideboard.

"Where *would* you go on holiday?" he asked.

"Lapland," I replied.

A glass of whisky came over my shoulder. "I put ginger ale in it," Geoffrey said.

"I'd go with him," Norman said.

"Could anyone go a sandwich?" Geoffrey asked. He pronounced it sang-gwitch. "I could go a jam butty." He emptied his half-tumblerful of the Irish whiskey and went down to the kitchen. In the shocking yellow light, I watched him pull open a cutlery drawer. The man that saw the great Tom Finney in action. The man that married Nora. He was small. From far away. Nothing special.

"What are you thinking?" Nora asked me. "You've gone very quiet."

I looked into the tawny brown trap of her eyes. "Oh, I was just . . ." I gestured at the chair in which I was sitting.

"Now don't get sad on me," she said. "Are you listening, boys?"

"It's just . . ."

"She was always here for us," Norman said. "Wasn't she, John Murdo? All our lives."

"Don't get sad, boys. She wouldn't want that."

After getting his Highers in the big school in Stornoway, Norman went to Glasgow University to become a bachelor of science. He was in Glasgow three weeks – the time it took him to drink his first term's grant in a pub called the Halt, on Woodlands Road. Then he came back home. He's been at home ever since. He's a quiet man. His voice never raised in the village. Nothing bothers him. If it's a fine day, he says, "Fine day." If it's raining, he says, "Wet."

Glasgow Rangers and rock-fishing. These are his interests.

"Do you want to see her?" he asked me.

"Yes, why not?" Nora was on her feet. "Geoffrey!" she shouted. "We're going through to see mum."

Geoffrey came into the kitchen doorway, a large morning roll in one hand, a tableknife clotted with red jam in the other. He'd just taken a large, quarter-moon bite out of the roll. "I won't bother," he said, chewing, his mouth full. He licked the blade of the knife. "Murr," he said.

We went through. Norman led the way. I let Nora go ahead of me. The coffin was set on trestles in the back bedroom. The lid was down.

"The best that money could buy!" Norman declared, patting the lid with the flat of his hand, before going round the coffin, unscrewing the brass bolts at the sides of the lid as he went. I wanted to tell him not to bother. Why was the lid down anyway? After unscrewing each bolt, he threw it on the bed, on top of the pink coverlet. Why not leave the lid off altogether? I waited for him to throw the coffin lid on top of the bed, after the bolts, but he carried it carefully in both hands and stood it against the wall, next to the door. He came back. "There she is," he said.

I looked into the coffin. Arrayed for the bridal in a white, satin shroud, ruched at the neck and hooded with a flap to go over her face, old Maggie Mary lay on padded silk, hands folded on her breast, eyes closed and her mouth, without false teeth, fallen open, a small, round, black hole. Why hadn't they closed her mouth properly? She reminded me of a piece of wedding cake you would get sent in a small, white box through the post. Nora was holding my hand in both her own. She was crying. Norman was gazing at me. I was expected to say something. "All our lives," I said. Norman nodded, relieved. "Well, well."

Nora sobbed and squeezed my hand.

"What's that smell?" I sniffed, and looked at Norman.

"That's what the undertaker sprays on them," Norman said. "Like air freshener."

I was expected to say something else.

"Well, well." Extricating my hand from Nora's, I placed it on old Maggie Mary's cold, folded hands. It wasn't her.

"Cheerio, Maggie," I said.

We went back to the livingroom, leaving Norman to replace the lid. Geoffrey was lying asleep on the couch, a hand under his head. He opened his eyes and sat up, blowing up his face out of the sides of his mouth and blinking up at Nora. "Bloody hell, love," he said, and sprang to his feet. "One more," he said, making for the sideboard and the bottles on it, "then I'm for me kip. Where's Norman?"

"He's coming," I said.

Geoffrey handed us our glasses, leaving Norman's on the sideboard. Raised his own half-tumblerful and made the small noise in his throat.

Down it went.

"You're some man, Geoffrey," I said. He looked at me unwinkingly, one side of his mouth ajar and a concentrated expression on his face, like a small side drummer I'd once seen in an army pipe band. I tried to shake hands with him.

"You're a man in a thousand, Geoffrey," I told him.

"Nat Lofthouse," he said.

"Yes, I . . ."

Geoffrey held his hand up: *sssh*!

"Nat Lofthouse. Centre forward. Bolton Wanderers and England."

"The Lion of Vienna," I said.

Geoffrey held his hand up.

"They didn't like playing against Nat," he said. "Centre halfs. He gave them a hard time, did Nat. Harold Johnston. Didn't want to play against Nat. None of them did. Going to me kip now," he said. "I know the way."

Off he went. "Going to me kip," I heard him telling Norman at the foot of the stairs. Norman came in. "What's wrong with Geoffrey?" he asked. "Why is he going to bed *now*?" "It's four in the morning," Nora said. "Is it?" Norman squinnied at the clock. "So it is. I'm going an' all." He went through, leaving his glass on the sideboard, undrunk.

"I'd better go too," I said to Nora.

"Finish your drink."

"Why not?"

"Have Norman's as well."

"Why ever not?"

"How are you feeling?"

"How are *you* feeling? Aren't you tired?"

She raised and lowered her eyebrows twice, rapidly – a trick she had, I remembered, from long ago. I drank my whisky – Norman's whisky – in one movement, Geoffrey-style, and stood up. I felt fine.

"Wait," she said. She went down to the kitchen and came back with my anorak. She had put on a thin, red jacket that matched the skirt. "Wait," she said again, and taking my unopened bottle of Grouse from the sideboard, put it in the pocket of the anorak. "You'll need this for the morning," she said. "Now put your arms into the arms." Opening out the anorak, she held it towards me.

"Where are *you* going?"

She was working her feet into strapless sandals. Gripping my arm for support.

"I'll see you home."

Hands on my shoulders, she propelled me from behind out of the livingroom and through the kitchen. She moved me as if in a dance: a conga for two. Her breath in my ear. I straightened the wooden condiment holder – *A Present from Yarmouth* – on the wall beside the kitchen door, Nora jigging with her feet behind me, switched off the kitchen light and opened the front door.

Outside, in the pre-dawn world, all was grey and still. We stood on the path, breathing in the raw, moist air. Two stars far down in the west, winking palely. Above the sooty finger of the Butt, where the morning would begin, dark purple clouds, massed and motionless, and no movement of waves breaking below. Sheep lying on the verges did not stir as we crossed the road; our feet did not disturb the silence.

"Ness, morning, very early," Nora said, behind me. "You gave me a crossbar home from a dance in Adabrock one time, on a morning like this."

"It wasn't my bike, it was Dolly Chalum's."

"Remember what we did when we got home?" Her finger poked into my back. "Over there. Where the peatstack was."

I opened the door of my house and went inside. The door closed behind me. Her feet followed me up into the livingroom.

I switched the light on and turned round. "Long time since you were in here," I said.

She glanced at me oddly, then looked round the room.

"Hmm . . ."

"No boom-boom joints in here," I told her. I took off my anorak, held up the bottle. She shook her head. "No," I continued, speaking very fast, "you won't find one nail in any of the woodwork in this room. All the old style. I had a job getting those beams for the ceiling, I can tell you. What do you think of my picture?"

"Yes, Norman said you were an artist . . ."

She went over to look at the watercolour of the *Toe of Galson at Sunset* above the mantelpiece.

"Well?"

"I like it."

"Is that all?"

"No, it's lovely."

"I made the frame as well."

Still looking at the picture, she took the red jacket off and dropped it on the floor. I bent down to retrieve it and her white blouse fell on my head. Straightening, clutching both garments, drowning, I saw her hand reach round and her shoulderblades move as she unclipped the brassiere at the back. It dropped to the floor as well. I went to pick it up, but she caught me by the wrists in a tight grip and held me there. I let the blouse and jacket fall and stared at her, my face pounding and trying to swallow down the thick sweetness in my throat. I couldn't speak. She smiled at me, raised and lowered her eyebrows; then, winding her right leg around my left, pressed against me and pulled my head down onto her breasts.

"Kiss them hello," she said.

Later, we lay on the carpet, not speaking. My mouth against her throat. Eyes closed. Her hand moved lightly on my back.

"I must go," she said.

I opened my eyes. She shook me.

"Are you asleep? Don't fall asleep."

"I'm not."

"Good." She sat up abruptly. "God, look at the time!" She started grabbing at her clothes, putting them on. I lay on my back, watching her. Relaxed in mind and body. Happy.

"You and me," I said.

"What about us?"

"We'd have been fine together."

"You think so?"

"Don't you?"

"We'll never know. Where the hell . . . ?" She found her skirt behind the sofa.

"You ever think what might have happened if we'd got married?"

"No."

"We should have got married, me and you."

"You never asked me."

"Would you have? If I'd asked?"

"What?"

"Married me?"

She sat back on her heels, buttoning the white blouse and looking down at me.

"Why are you asking that?"

"I don't know."

"Why are you asking that now?"

"I don't know."

"Of course I would," she said. "I loved you."

I wanted to ask her something else, but she put her hand up: *sssh*! as Geoffrey had done earlier.

"You were so full of yourself after I let you. You wouldn't believe it was my first time, and you knew I'd let you again, any time you wanted, because I loved you, I was a real goner for you, head over heels, and once you knew that it made you even more proud and you wouldn't have anything to do with me, you ignored me, except when you wanted the one thing, and you told everybody, all your pals, yes you did, even that horrible creature out in the moor, only for fear of my father he'd have been in my window and in my bed, and you were the real cock of the walk in this village for a while, weren't you? The cock of the north. That was you."

She bent down and kissed me on the mouth.

"Why are you so afraid all the time?" she asked. "All your life? That's no way to live." She rubbed her forehead against mine. "What we did just now. Wasn't it lovely? Hmm? What is there to be afraid of?"

"I'm not afraid," I said. "What do you mean, I'm afraid?"

As abruptly as she'd sat up, she jumped to her feet. Pushing a foot into one of the sandals, she clattered over to where the other one was on its face beside the television set, kicked it the right way up and shoved her other foot into it. I lay on my side, my head on my crossed arms, my face averted from her. I felt the toe of a sandal poking me in the back.

"You should have gone to Spain," she said.

Naked, I stood at the window, and watched through a gap in the curtains as she crossed the road and started up the path to their house; walking quickly and carrying the thin red jacket in one hand. Why hadn't she put it on? Her tights were in one of the pockets. From the way she was hurrying, I thought she would go straight into the house without a backward glance, but she didn't, she stopped in the doorway as though she'd remembered something, stood with her back to me, jigging her feet, then turned and waved to me. And when she did that I knew that my luck had run out and that my life was over, that it would all be against me from now on, that my sobriety was a sham, my watercolours no good, my oak panellings and false ceilings in vain, that my beams would collapse, my tiles crack, my house crumble and fall, my wife go away, my daughter be elsewhere, and that they would have no luck either, none at all, ever. All this I knew, plain as glass, clear as currents on the surface of the ocean, as from the threshold of her house old Maggie Mary, laughing, waved, beckoned to me, *O you Satan!* a fresh breeze agitating her shroud and the sun, two hours too early, from the wrong part of the sky, shining on her.

I remember it as if it was yesterday. I was passing the manse in my sailor's uniform, and the minister, Mr Macaulay, came out in his cardigan and slippers, no collar, and said, "Come into my study, Roderick", full of books, and he made a long prayer unto the Lord, and he said, " A thousand at thy side shall fall, on thy right hand shall lie, ten thousand dead; yet unto thee, it shall not once come nigh . . ." and he took me by the hand and said, "You shall return, Roderick, as you are leaving," meaning alive. And I did, without a scratch, it was the truth he told me, apart from falling down a hatch in one ship I was on and splitting my head open. But that had nothing to do with the war. How I lost the eye is another story.

The Lost Sheep

I drove up the brae and turned right at the top into the old quarry. It wasn't yet eight o'clock. Two other cars, one with a green tent pitched beside it, were in there before me. I didn't see anyone. I got out of the car (hired from a garage in Stornoway) and locked it. Even this early, there was the feel of a hot day. The village was two hundred yards further down the road.

I walked along in my black suit and tie, carrying my coat over my left arm. Six years since I'd been home. The land hadn't changed. There was the Atlantic, in the distance, on one side of the road. The moor was on the other side. I walked along. The morning was grey and still. I couldn't get over the silence.

The sprawl of council houses at the entrance to the village hadn't been there six years ago. Smoke from one chimney went straight up into the air. It wasn't peat smoke. I would have to walk the length of the village to get to where I was going – the house my brother had built was on a plot of ground belonging to the family at the far end of the village, near the river. After teaching in Glasgow for thirty years, he'd taken early retirement, gone back home and built himself a large house with many windows, a barn at the back, and a garage. He'd bought a fishing boat. A tractor. He'd turned over the rough ground at the front of the house to make a garden. He was building a drystone wall. Not the most welcoming of hosts whenever I visited him in his spotless flat in the West End of Glasgow, he would have a good excuse today for not rising to greet me when I arrived on his doorstep – he was in a coffin in one of the downstairs bedrooms. At one o'clock this afternoon, after "the books", we would carry him out of the

large new house he'd built for himself, and in which he'd lived
for almost three months, take him on a bier as far as the bridge
and thence, in a hearse, to the district cemetery. And there, in a
lair that already contained his father and his mother, we would
leave him.

A strange-looking dog – spotted like a Dalmatian, but with a
head like a greyhound – barked at me from the gate of Waldo's
house as I passed; I heard a high, English voice calling to it to be
quiet and come in here. Our old family house – number three
– was down from Waldo's, on the moorland side of the road.
After my mother's death six years ago, my sister had put the
house on the market, sold it to the highest bidder – a retired
doctor from Northumberland – and moved into one of the
Swedish houses on the New road. How she contrived to do
this, I don't know. I think she registered herself as homeless
with the council. Perhaps she claimed a special dispensation
from the housing department for herself and her husband, a
dissolute semi-invalid from Whiteinch. For two years after
that, she was never off the mainland – the first hint of a
seasonal sale or grand opening would find her hot-foot in
Inverness, in Perth, in Glasgow, staying in licensed hotels
and going round the shops; the semi-invalid from Whiteinch
skipping after her like a spring lamb, when he wasn't dodging
in taxicabs to the nearest British Legion or Rangers Supporters'
Club. Until the money ran out . . . The walls of the old house
were now whitewashed, the window frames painted a bright
red, new slates were on the roof, a satellite dish against one
of the chimneys, and a name – *Benview* – embedded in black
lettering on a shiny wooden board on the gate. Waldo's house,
I had noticed in passing, also had a new name – *Tigh na Sith*
– which in Gaelic means "House of Peace". I could hear the
high English voice saying it. Another house in the village was
called *Tigh na Fois*, which means "House of Rest. The family
in that house was from Birmingham.

By the time I'd reached the middle of the village, where the
shop, storehouse, barn and byre of the biggest merchant in the

district used to stand (all gone, as though they'd never been) the sun had started to break through the grey haze, catch the cups and wires on the tops of the telegraph poles, and glint on the windows of the houses facing seawards. It was going to be a hot one all right. From here, it was downhill all the way. I passed *Oceanview* and *Ceol na Mara*. Only two of the houses in this half of the village were still occupied by the original families. The rest were incomers. They weren't all English. Some were Lowland Scots. One was German. I could understand them – I thought – settling in those parts of the Highlands and Islands – Skye, for example, or Wester Ross – where there is scenery. But what had brought them to this flat, treeless, windswept lawn between a rock and a bog in the far north of Lewis, traversed by electric and telegraph poles, tar roads and rylock fences – strewn with sheepshit, abandoned wrecks of cars, empties – where the dominant building is the Free Church of Scotland, and where it rains for seven months of the year? I rounded the glebe corner at the bottom of the east end brae and my brother's house, previously seen only in photographs, came into view for the first time, in the glen below. There it was. The house that John built. It was even bigger than I'd expected. Dark-glazed, diamond-leaded bay windows, surmounted by overlapping red tiles; at the front, three pitched-roof dormer windows, also leaded, on the roof, an arched wooden trellis round the front door, and another framework against the wall at one side, up which, as I came closer, I saw an ivy beginning to climb. It wasn't like an island house at all. The barn at the back looked very white and very new. The garage likewise. He'd been a busy man, my brother. It was the last house in the village. Carry on beyond the barn and you came to the river. The low, wrought-iron gate swung open at a touch without squealing, then closed itself behind me. A straight path of polished granite slabs led up to the front door. Try keeping your feet on that on a frosty winter's night. My left knee was hurting badly. I should have taken the car all the way to the house. But I had wanted to see the village. I had wanted to feel something. The plant at the side of the house wasn't an ivy but a clematis. I stood on the red-tiled front doorstep, under the trellis, taking deep breaths, until the hissing in my ears stopped. Then I opened the door and went in.

A woman with a round, fat face, wearing a brown nylon overall and yellow rubber gloves, came out of what was (presumably) the kitchen and saw me standing in the porch. Her eyes went round and her mouth fell open.

"Hello, Mary Ann."

"Oh ghraidh . . ."

She came down the hallway in a clumsy rush, bumping against a small table with a telephone on it, pulling off the rubber gloves as she came. Holding the gloves in one hand, she put her arms round me and gave me a hug. The front of her overall was damp.

"Ghraidh a ghraidh . . ."

"Heeesht now, Mary Ann." I patted her on the back, awkwardly, and then on the top of the head. She had short, springy black hair, tightly curled. It was like patting a pot scourer. "Come on, now . . ."

"Yes, yes." She let me go and looked intently up into my face. She started crying. "Who expected this?" she wailed. "Who ever thought?"

"I know," I said.

"Ghraidh a ghraidh . . ."

"I know."

She was my second cousin on my father's side. She was the first to let me try her – not in a bed but in a field of newly-stooked corn, beneath the light of the moon that ripens the barley. I was fourteen, she was thirteen. It had been a disaster. "Lord, how he trembles!" she'd exclaimed at one stage, exasperated. "There's no one here, only Agnes," she told me, wiping her eyes. Agnes was my sister. "The rest of them went home earlier." By the rest of them, she meant the mourners who had sat up all night with the corpse.

"Where is she?" I asked Mary Ann.

"Agnes? She's upstairs," Mary Ann replied. "She went to bed as soon as I appeared."

"She's sleeping *here*?"

"Poor thing, she's taking it very badly." Mary Ann took my coat and hung it on a hook in the porch. "She's been here since John died. She won't go back to her own house for anyone. Stewie, Marjorie, your uncle Willie. They've all tried. She refuses to budge." Her voice dropped to a whisper. "Will I wake her up and tell her you're here?"

"No," I said.

We went through to the kitchen. Pine units, white worktops. Glossy parquet floor. White walls. Everything very bright, very new. A long neon tube in the ceiling. I sat on one of the high wooden stools and Mary Ann started filling an electric kettle at the sink. She filled it through the spout. "What am I thinking?" she sobbed, above the rush of the tap. "He came back from Inverness in a closed coffin. A massive heart attack, the post mortem said." She turned off the tap and plugged in the kettle. A little red light appeared at its base. "Do you want to see the coffin?" she sobbed. "It's the second door along."

"Maybe later."

"Your own brother," she sobbed, "and you can't take a last look at him."

I thought of something.

"It doesn't matter, Mary Ann," I said. "I'd rather remember him as he was."

"You're right." She wiped her eyes on a piece of paper towel, then loudly blew her nose into it. "So then," she said. "Have you eaten anything today? Will I make you ham and eggs?"

"Tea will be fine."

"Better eat something."

Through the kitchen window, beyond the bridge and the first of the unworked village peat banks, I could see the moor in her summer hues of brown and green and purple, stretching out to the horizon. The ben, which, on my walk through the village, had been a shadowy grey outline, was now pale blue and sharp against the skyline. The river had very little water in it; between flat, shallow pools, the river bed was dry. The kitchen filled with white light. Mary Ann moved steadily between the cooker and the fridge. With a fish slice, she pushed pieces of bacon around in a frying pan. She put a mug of milky tea and a sugarbowl with the spoon in it on the breakfast bar in front of me. "Drink that," she said. Steadily, in the white light, the red second hand on the kitchen wall clock moved round the dial. My left leg ached. To ease the pain, I stretched it out straight underneath the table. ". . . all morning," Mary Ann was saying. "Cathy Dods is coming at eleven to help me with the dinner. And Red's wife, and Joan." Something in the cooker went ding. I thought of my brother, two doors along, dead. How could anyone be dead on a day like this?

"Here," said Mary Ann, putting a plate of bacon and eggs and fried bread in front of me. "There's more tea in the pot." She looked at me. "Maybe you'd like something in it?"

"I've stopped."

She kept looking at me.

"Since when?"

"Three years."

"That *is* news," she said. "Do you miss it at all?"

"Every day. And every night."

"I wish *my* amadan would stop." She put her hand to her mouth. "Listen to me in the house of the dead!"

"How *is* Donald John?"

"Don't ask."

Behind me, the kitchen door opened.

"Ah yes," a voice huffed tremulously. "You're here at last, are you?" I didn't need to turn round to know who it was. Shuffle shuffle went what sounded like leather slippers on the parquet floor and my sister, in a pink, wadded housecoat open at the front to reveal a creased purple slip, the hair standing out from her head like a madwoman's, mouth twisted to one side and real tears in her eyes, appeared at the end of the table, gesturing wordlessly at me. She turned to Mary Ann, and Mary

Ann seemed to know the routine, for she put an arm round her, coaxed her into a chair beside the cooker, fetched a bottle of whisky and a glass from one of the cupboards, half-filled the glass with whisky and asked my sister did she want water in it, to which enquiry my sister, still staring at me, wordlessly shook her head. Mary Ann then crossed over to the chair, half-knelt, and again putting her arm round my sister, held the glass to her lips. Taking little, shuddering sips, my sister emptied the glass. "No one knows," she told Mary Ann in a huffing, quavering little voice. "I have to do everything. No one helps me." Tears ran down her face. "No one understands how much I've suffered. How much I'm suffering. No one." She allowed Mary Ann to help her to her feet and back across the kitchen towards the door.

"You try and get a sleep, a ghraidh," Mary Ann said softly, "before people start arriving." The shuffling came to a brief halt behind my back. "No one," my sister's voice quavered. The shuffling started again. She went out.

I work in London. Once I'd settled my late brother's affairs – which would take a couple of days – I would be going back there. I like the big city. I started out in London as a civil servant at the age of eighteen; now I work as a consultant for various companies. I have my own office and secretary, and a house in Ealing. I could never come back to Lewis to live. I don't even come back on holidays. If I have to come back, as now, I prefer to stay in Stornoway, in a hotel. My house in Ealing is so big, I rent it out as bedsits, and live myself in a self-contained flat in the basement. I find that Pakistanis make the best tenants. I used to take students, but too many of them attempted suicide on my premises, after failing their exams. Of our family, only my sister married. I suppose I could have married Mary Ann once; she had a great fancy for me, in spite of my poor performance among the sheaves. She used to write to me when I first went to London; long gossipy letters, half in English, half in Gaelic, on headed, lined blue paper from the Dreadnought Hotel, Callander (where she worked as a cook);

full of misspellings and grammatical errors and totally devoid of punctuation. I have them to this day.

"What did I tell you?" she said, coming back in. "She's taking it very badly, the soul. I only hope the turns don't come back, that she used to have before your mother died."

"Ah yes, the turns," I said. "I remember the turns. I think we were all privileged to witness at least one of the turns." Mary Ann shook her head sorrowfully at me. I went to say something else, and just then the first cars started to pull up outside the house.

"Who was that minister?" I asked my cousin Angus.

"Macphail?" said Angus. "He's from Harris, I think."

"Praying in English at the graveside. I couldn't believe my ears."

"His Gaelic isn't very good," said Mary Ann, "that's the reason. But he's a nice man."

"What's he doing in a church in this district if he can't speak Gaelic?"

"His parents were from Harris," my cousin Murdo said. "But he was brought up in Glasgow. That's how he hasn't got the Gaelic."

"He's a Glasgow Highlander," said Angus.

"He's got some Gaelic," Donald John said. "He preaches in Gaelic."

"Once a month," said Angus. "On a Wednesday evening."

"He feels he can put his message across better in English," said cousin Murdo's wife, Ishbel. "And he's a nice man. The people here like him, especially the young. And what's it to any of *you*," she said then, "whether he preaches in Gaelic or German, who never darken the door of a church anyway?"

We were back in the house. Long tables covered with white cloths had been set up in two rooms, and the big post-funeral dinner was in full swing. All the neighbours and most of our relations were present, including a contingent from Uig I remembered from six years ago – two tall, silent brothers, their sister and the sister's tall, silent husband – who only appeared at funerals and who, installed at one end of the large table in the livingroom, and having already succeeded in demolishing two entire gigots of mutton between them, were now seriously engaged over a yellow baking bowl of trifle, the sister exhorting the men, between mouthfuls, with subdued Uig grunts, to try more of this, take another spoonful of that. She had refused all offers of drink on their behalf except a water jug, a prejudice shared by few others in the company, and the whisky, sherry and wine bottles on a side table were in constant demand.

I sat in the place I had chosen for myself at the smaller table in the livingroom, between cousin Angus and Donald John, Mary Ann's husband, and across from my cousin Murdo from Habost and his wife Ishbel. I should have been at the big table, along with my sister, who, clad in dark mainland finery and smiling a smile that turned up the corners of her mouth, seemed to have recovered from the modest (by her standards) morning fit of hysterics and a later, more spectacular fit, preceded by loud, startling ululations, as the coffin was being carried out of the house; her husband Stewie, already rendered more or less incoherent by drink; their daughter Marjorie and her four children; and old Uncle Willie, my father's brother, gabbling incessantly from his place of honour at the opposite end of the table from the Uigeachs, and pausing only to throw his head back from time to time and oscillate his Adam's apple in a barking laugh at something he himself had just said, or raise to his mouth, with a shaking, liver-spotted hand, a large tumbler of whisky. The girls serving at the tables all gave him a wide berth, in case he tried to put his hand up their skirts. It came to me that perhaps, behind their doors, all families were as awful as mine. Sipping a watery still orange, I conned the live faces around me, eating and drinking and talking, getting louder and livelier by the minute, and thought of the one whose house we were in, two miles away, at the beginning of his death, silent under the fine earth of the machair. Already beginning to be forgotten. In the room next door, chairs were being scraped back as people stood up, preparing to leave. Some came into the doorway to say their farewells. "You're not going *yet*?" my sister kept repeating. Feet started tramping out in the hall; the front door began to open and close. A tractor roared into life in Sandy's park across the river. "Be fine," I heard a voice say, "if I didn't have to be over at the Crofters by five." The world getting its dungarees on and back into gear. The funeral was over.

"Never mind that," Angus said, "why haven't they made you Lord Mayor of London yet?" and the others laughed. They wouldn't be going home for some time yet. Drink was on the go, and they had their suits on. The wives would go away and come back for them. The Uig cousins at the other table wouldn't be in any hurry to leave either. Not until they had ascertained that the patterns on the pudding plates couldn't be scraped off and eaten.

"I was in London plenty times," Donald John told me. "When I was sailing."

"The New Zealand Shipping Company," said Murdo. "Who wasn't?"

"Don't talk to *me* about London," said Donald John.

"Yes," Angus said, "but the London you were in and the London I was in . . . dockside boozers and the like . . . is not the same as . . ." He stopped.

"As what?" I asked.

"You know. Posh London. Where *you* are. Cocktails. That woman with the teeth on the telly."

"I was in a bar in the West End of London once," Murdo said. "It was full of poofs and lawyers."

"Oh, be quiet with your mouth," Mary Ann told Murdo, and from the other side of the table Ishbel added, "Who on this day of days wants to hear where you were in London or Mesopotamia or anywhere else on earth?"

They'd been round the world, the three of them; not once but many times. On merchant navy ships. Murdo had been a bo'sun, the other two ABs, although Donald John also sailed sometimes as ship's carpenter. On land, on sea, there was nothing they couldn't turn their hands to. They could build houses. Weave tweeds. Slaughter and butcher sheep. Angus was skipper of a fishing boat out of Stornoway. They were older than I was. Murdo used to give John and myself haircuts when we were small – if you didn't keep your head still, he would give you a rap on top of your skull with the clippers to remind you. And I remembered how, as a schoolboy in Stornoway, I used to see them on Cromwell Street in their grey, square-shouldered gaberdine raincoats, belted about the middle (Murdo usually wearing a hat) and carrying large, brown suitcases, bound for another trip deep-sea to faraway places with strange-sounding names, and how I used to envy them; and how, on their return – brown-faced , clean and manly, rolling Capstan bonded navy cut tobacco into ticklers – I would ask them about places they'd been to and hear about waterfront grogshops and six o'clock swills and what the whores were like. I once asked Donald John – he was talking about Vancouver – if he'd been to the zoo there. "What zoo?" he said. Here they were, looking as if they'd never been further from home than a ram sale in Dingwall. I didn't envy them now. Two hours from now, I would be back in my hotel room in Stornoway. Two days from now, I would be back in my house in London. They would still be here. They'd never really left. They'd gone round the world and seen the sea and come back to become their own fathers.

"Onassis," a voice said at my elbow, and Uncle Willie swam into my ken like a creature from another element, breathed on me and sat smartly on the floor. "*Ark – ark – ark*," he went, as a small scramble of women, holding tightly onto his arms, assisted him to his feet and sat him on a chair beside me. Mary Ann fetched his tumbler of whisky from the other table. "Now behave yourself," she told him. Without looking at her, he tried to put his hand up her skirt. He was staring at me, beady-eyed. "How are things in the great wen?" he asked, and threw back his head with a barking laugh.

"Good one, Willie," said Donald John.

"*Ark – ark – ark*," went Uncle Willie. He took a shaky sip of whisky from the tumbler. "Anything fresh in Putney?" he asked. "How are they all keeping in Tooting Bec?"

"Good one," said Donald John again, automatically.

"Your mother," Uncle Willie began. "A corner of whose coffin, if I'm not mistaken, I saw sticking out when I looked into that hole today. You can't get the gravediggers up here anymore. *Ark – ark – ark*. Now your mother should never have married your father. My brother John. That the recent late lamented was named after. No . . ." he looked round the table. "She should have married me."

"You're starting," said Mary Ann.

"I liked John," Uncle Willie continued. "Your brother." He prodded me in the ribs. "He was odd. Kept taking baths. Thought Ben Jonson was greater than Shakespeare. But I liked him. He wasn't rich, like you. He always brought his uncle Willie a forty ouncer when he came home. And two hundred fags. Everything that's bad for you. But not bad for your uncle Willie. You're not drinking, I notice. You'll be richer than ever. Ark – ark – ark. I loved your mother with all my heart." He breathed on me again. "And you're not really rich, you know. You're poor. Even if you're rich, you're poor. You're a dodger." He looked over to the other table. "The poor mouth will be wanting to waylay you before you scuttle off. Talk high finance. Dodge that one if you can. Why is my glass empty?"

"I'll get it." Mary Ann was on her feet. "Sorry," she mouthed.

"What for?" Donald John asked her.

"I wasn't talking to you," Mary Ann said.

"Why don't you take her to London with you?" Donald John said to me. "Give us all a bit of peace?"

"*Ark – ark – ark*," went Uncle Willie, and prodded me in the ribs.

"What are you saying, boy?" Mary Ann stared down at Donald John. "Have you lost your senses?"

"Take it easy, D.J.," said Murdo.

"Go to London and see the queen," said Donald John.

"Go to London *with* the queen," said Uncle Willie. "*Ark – ark – ark.*"

"All family here," Angus spoke rapidly on the other side of me. "No more nonsense, that'll do."

"On this day of days," said Ishbel.

"*Ark – ark – ark.*"

"See what you've started now!" Mary Ann accused Uncle Willie.

"He started nothing," Donald John muttered. His face was red.

"No, but I'll finish something," Murdo said, "if he doesn't drop it right now." Making a quick circular motion with his hand, index finger pointing downwards, he signalled to the girls at the small side table: *Fill them up.*

"You promised me you wouldn't," Ishbel hissed at him.

"Of course," Uncle Willie turned his beady eye on me again, "there's a history of sexual . . . what's the euphemism? . . . *neutrality* on one side of our family . . ." but before he could get any further Murdo had stretched across the table and caught hold of him by the wrist.

"Willie," he said. "How would you like to be taken home bodily and put to bed with a glass of water and a gingersnap?"

Uncle Willie bleared at him. "Can I have a pisspot?"

"Right." Murdo started to get to his feet. But he was grinning.

"Murdo, son of Angus, son of my Aunt Murdina." Uncle Willie pretended to be alarmed. "You wouldn't, would you?"

"He would and he will." Mary Ann dumped a half-full tumbler of whisky next to his hand. "You wait, boy," she told Donald John.

"Where's his respect for grey hairs?" Uncle Willie took a shaky, rattling gulp of the whisky, spilling some down his chin and shirt front. "Does the Old Testament count for nothing in the house of Murdo, son of Angus, son of my Aunt Murdina, the egg-stealer and knitter of bobban long johns with bone buttons for the flyholes?"

"Oh, what's the use of talking to him!" Ishbel exclaimed, letting out a yelp of laughter and then immediately putting a hand over her mouth.

He'd been a teacher as well, my Uncle Willie; not in schools, in universities; not therefore a teacher, a lecturer. Speaking of him, the wise people in the district would say, *A brilliant man gone to the dogs*, lowering their voices and shaking their heads as they said it. At the start of his career, he'd studied for the ministry in the Church of Scotland (the family were Free Church) and came out as a doctor of divinity and ordained minister of the gospel, but packed all that in when, as he used to tell *ad nauseum*, he lost his faith and his virginity together one night to a fat harlot in Falkirk. On the same night, the fat harlot also converted him to communism. The road to Damascus in reverse. After that, he went to Edinburgh University, graduated with first class Honours in English and Celtic, was immediately taken on by the English department as a research fellow and part-time lecturer, published a book of critical essays entitled *The Fool in the Loft*, moved to Glasgow as a full-time lecturer and published a book on the Jacobean dramatists (chiefly John Webster) which is still used as a set text in universities and caused a famous academic controversy between Uncle Willie and a professor in the Antipodes. Did he go to Trinity College, Dublin, for two years? I know he was back in Edinburgh, in a post created for him in the School of Scottish Studies, the time he came down to London, at the invitation of the Gaelic Society of London, to give a lecture on the poetry of the '45 Rebellion, and I went along to hear him. The hall was full of men in kilts and dinner jackets and women with permed hair and long white dresses (a ceilidh and dance was to follow the lecture) and from the way one ginger-haired bluffer (who, not content with making a public exhibition of himself in full Highland dress, also had some kind of heavy medalled chain around his neck) kept disappearing behind the platform, reappearing and gesticulating hopelessly at a rival sartorial stag in the front row, I gathered that all was not well behind the scenes and that something was up with the guest of honour. I wasn't wrong. The ginger-haired man had barely launched into an apology for the non-appearance of the distinguished lecturer and scholar, due to an unforeseen and, hopefully, temporary indisposition, when the curtains behind him were violently agitated and Uncle Willie's head, followed by the rest of Uncle Willie's body, suddenly burst into view. He swayed for a few seconds, clinging to the curtains, orientating himself, then high-stepped to the front of the platform as confidently as a young cockerel. With his skinny neck, beaky nose, bright beady eyes and hair combed back and standing up on his head, he didn't look unlike a cockerel. He had a moustache. Calling for a chair to be handed up to him, and waving the ginger-haired man off the stage, he sat down, produced a half-bottle of whisky from the inside pocket of his tweed jacket, took a swig, went "Pah!" and replaced the bottle inside his jacket. "Charles Edward Louis John Casimir Sylvester Severino Maria . . ." he intoned, and he was off. He spoke for two hours, without notes, and no one moved. He went on a historical and literary excursus. You wanted him to go on forever. He had the poems and songs of the '45 off by heart. Some of the songs he sang. He recited the poems in Gaelic first, then translated them into English. The half-bottle stayed in his inside pocket. At the end of two hours, he stood up abruptly and stomped to the back of the stage, violently agitating the curtains for a second time looking for the way out. The audience were so entranced they forgot to clap until he'd disappeared. That was Uncle Willie, once upon a time. The ginger-haired man ran offstage after him, clapping furiously, to try and make him come back out, but nothing doing. Asked by the same man, not long into the ceilidh-dance, to take Uncle Willie away, I found myself accompanying him to an Irish bar in Tottenham, where he seemed to know a lot of people with pork pie hats and fine cement dust in their eyebrows; to an Irish house in Muswell Hill, where he sat up all night drinking and talking Irish Gaelic; and finally to an early-morning market pub, with a garrulous rabble of Irishmen in tow, before I managed to put him on a train back to Edinburgh at King's Cross. He had no luggage. Some of the Irishmen wanted to get on the train with him. "The grim reaper," a voice groaned above my head – it was one of the Uig cousins – to which Uncle Willie responded, "The happy sower," before being shushed by several female voices. "William," the Uigeach, who was known as Donald the Elder, said, shaking his head – then, to me, "This is a time of sorrow. Words are weak. What we have is the hope and belief that the dear one taken so suddenly from our midst is even now in a better place."

"He's in the ground," said Uncle Willie. "We're just done putting him there."

"William," the Uigeach said again – then, to me, "May God be with you and with all of you at this time. We must go. No . . ." he forestalled my sister's protest, ". . . we must. You must come and visit with us," he said to me, "if you have time, before you go back to the city."

"I will," I said.

"We will look forward to that," said the Uigeach. "Now we must go. The coats," he told his sister, who, with gently puffing cheeks and a shine of sweat on her upper lip, seemed to have taken root between the tables. She pouted at him but made no move.

"I'll get them," said Mary Ann. "I know where they are."

In the silence that followed, the other Uig cousin, known as Donald the Deacon, sighed out loud.

"Yir rye therr, pal," my sister's husband, Stewie, slurred up at him. Silence. I found myself staring at Donald John. Mary Ann appeared in the doorway with the coats.

"Ye-es . . ." Donald the Elder said to no one in particular. "Goodbye," he said. He held out his hand. I shook it. He shook hands with Donald John and Angus and Murdo and Ishbel.

Donald the Deacon didn't bother. Neither did the sister or the sister's husband.

"William," said Donald the Elder.

"Goodbye to you," said Uncle Willie.

"Thank God for that," said Donald John, as he watched them going out, followed by my sister.

"Heesht," said Ishbel, "before they hear you." She looked towards the door and then at her hand, working the fingers. "Some grip he had," she said.

"I'll have to be going too." I made a pretence of looking at my watch.

"Where?" said Murdo. "Aren't you staying over?"

"*Ark*," said Uncle Willie.

"No," I said. "A lot to do in Stornoway tomorrow, so . . ."

"Agnes!" Uncle Willie shouted.

"Stay over with ourselves," Angus urged me. "Man alive!"

"What?" My sister's face appeared in the doorway.

"He says he's going," Uncle Willie told her. "*Ark – ark – ark.*"

"Who?" My sister frowned. "Bed here for you," she said.

"When do we ever see you?" said Angus. "Man alive!"

"No," I stood up. "I have to go."

"Urgent appointments," said Uncle Willie.

"Something like that."

"The loneliest always have the most urgent appointments." I sat down again.

"How's the novel going, Willie?" I asked him. "Still at it, I hope? How long is it now since we first heard about the great work in progress? Twenty-five years? Thirty? Nearer thirty, I would say. So is she coming to a point? – as old grand-uncle Norman used to say. When can we expect an announcement in all the literary supplements? People in Putney and Tooting Bec keep stopping me in the street and asking. They're getting impatient and you can't really blame them. I mean, time's getting on. There must be a small Amazon rainforest of manuscript up there in your house by now, covered with your spooky handwriting. Does J.D. Salinger know he has a rival? Still, it'll be worth the wait, once it appears. I know it's a masterpiece because you told me it was, and I believe you. I've got it from the horse's mouth. Any nearer to getting a title for it, by the way? James Joyce had the same problem with *Finnegans Wake*. And Thackeray with *Vanity Fair*. You, Joyce and Thackeray. Someday, someone will write a thesis. I'd do it myself, only I'm so busy making money these days, and unlike you I don't know enough about great literature to make comparative judgements. What if you're greater than Joyce? What if this unfinished, untitled masterpiece of yours is greater than *Ulysses*? I couldn't say that without being accused of bias and nepotism. He's talking of his Uncle Willie here, they'd say, the fierce London critics. Well . . ." I stood up. "I won't keep you from your desk any longer, uncle of mine. I really have to go." My voice started stammering; I felt tears at the back of my eyes, the way he was looking at me. But he'd started it. "Keep at it," I stammered. "Wouldn't presume to dictate to a great artist, but all that stuff about my mother is material for the novel, surely, not for drunken dissipation around a dinner table? You'll know yourself. It's your territory and you're in control of it. Anyone can see that. Goodbye now," I stammered. "My money's on you."

In the hall, I asked a girl with big, dark-brown eyes: "Is there a bathroom downstairs?"

"I'll show you," she said. I followed her along the passage-way.

"Are you Mary Ann's girl?" I asked her. "You look like her."

"Donald John's girl, yes. Here it is," she said.

"You look like your mother," I told her.

"Oh *no!*" she said. "*Everyone* says that!"

"Which one are you? Katie?"

"Fiona Mairi."

"Well, Fiona Mairi, you look lovely and thanks very much."

"You're welcome."

In the bathroom, I sat with my face in my hands – the bowl I was sitting on had a smaller bowl with a foot pedal beside it, a bidet it was called. Now what salesman had persuaded him he needed one of these? A vein in the side of my forehead throbbed under my fingers. I was crying. After a while, I stood up and flushed the bowl, then washed my hands and face in cold water at the basin and dried them on a big, fleecy bathtowel hanging over a rail. I looked at my face in the mirror. Uncle Willie's face looked back at me. You're not the only one who's read a book, I told him. You're not the only one with a tongue in his head. My face frowned back at me. Feeling all right again, I opened the door of the bathroom.

"Ah, there you are!" my sister said.

Since her early-morning performance for my benefit, my sister had undergone several personality changes. Now, in the declining afternoon, she was the dignified, reasonable, slow-speaking matron. Smilimg the smile that turned up the corners of her mouth, she laid a gentle, restraining hand on my sleeve.

"How can you leave us so soon, your own family? Poor Marjorie, you haven't even spoken to her."

"Hallo, Marjorie." Marjorie smiled at me. She had a baby in her arms.

"So what's the name of this one?"

"Ludovic."

"And the father?"

"From Uist. But he lives in Alness."

"What's on your mind, Agnes?" I turned to my sister.

"Not here." She went into a bedroom. I followed her.

"You stay out there," she told Marjorie. Marjorie smiled at me again. She was a pale, happy lank of a girl who never contradicted anybody. My sister closed the door.

"We have to talk."

"What about?"

"Well. Did he leave a will? I have a right to know."

"Sure."

"What's in it, if it isn't a big secret?"

"I don't know."

"We put a lot of work into this house, myself and Stewie."

"I didn't know that."

"All the wallpapering. I did that. And Stewie was labouring for him, on and off, when his back would let him. For nothing."

"Doesn't sound like John."

"What?"

"Not paying people."

"I'm telling you."

"Tell the lawyer. He's handling all claims on the estate."

"But you're the trustee. The beneficiary."

"What do you want, Agnes?"

"For myself, nothing. But I have the interests of my daughter to consider."

"Marjorie?"

"You know what she's like. No home, no man. Four of a family now."

"I thought she had a home in Alness."

"A council house."

"Well, *you* chose to live in a council house. What's the problem?"

"You know what Marjorie's like. She's a bit simple. Easily led."

"She's of age. She must know what she wants by now."

"And Alness is a bad place to bring up children. Ask Stewie. It's wild."

"But you once told me that Marjorie loved it there. Didn't she refuse a bigger council house in Tain?"

"Marjorie needs to be near her mother. Those children need a grandmother."

"Are you planning to move to Alness, then?"

She looked away from me, towards the window, and said quickly, "I think Marjorie should have this house."

"Is that why you've already taken up occupancy?"

"No." Still looking away, she said, "John told me to stay. He came to me in a dream the night he died. 'Stay in the house, Agnes,' he said. 'Don't leave the house empty.'"

"That's interesting," I told the back of her head. "I'd tell that dream to the lawyer if I were you, see where it stands as hearsay evidence. In the meantime . . ." She turned round. The reasonable matron had gone; a creature with narrowed eyes, a quivering, mottled chin and a straight line for a mouth had taken her place. ". . . I'd go back to your own house. Back to Stewie."

"What about this house?"

"Not your problem."

"Why can't Marjorie have it? His niece. Keep it in the family."

"He gave you a house once. His sister. Keep it in the family."

"That was different."

Suddenly I felt very clear-headed.

"He didn't want to. But, at least, he consoled himself, the house would be staying in the family. Wrong again. Your mother is barely a month in the ground when long-lost Stewie turns up from wherever he's been, grinning all over his pan and carrying all his worldly goods in a black bin liner. It isn't a flying visit. He's back to stay. After a botched attempt to burn down the kitchen in order to get a new one on the insurance and a scam involving a car which ends with him getting his jaw broken by a Westsider, you put the house – our family home – on the market. Will I go on? Now you want this house for your daughter Marjorie. But what if it turns out to be like mother like daughter? What if Marjorie sells John's second house as quickly as you sold the first one?"

"She won't."

"You're right she won't."

"You hate me, don't you?"

"Why do you say that?"

"You hate everyone."

"Not true, Agnes."

"I heard you in there with Uncle Willie. I know what you were doing."

"What I'm doing now is leaving. Mary Ann is caretaker of the house. I've asked her to lock up as soon as the party's over. If you have a set of keys, leave them with her. Oh, a man from the lawyer's in Stornoway will be over tomorrow to do an inventory. And a copy of John's will – those parts of it relevant to yourself – will come through your letterbox in due course. I think that's all for the time being. Unless there's something else you want to discuss?"

"Hate, hate, hate . . ."

"I don't hate you, Agnes. We're family. As well hate a scorpion for having a sting."

"What do you mean by that?"

"It's our nature. We can't help it. Now, who do you suppose is the soberest of the relations? I'm needing a lift to the old quarry . . ."

Ishbel put her head out of the car window.

"We never see you at home anymore," she said, "except at funerals. London must be a wonderful place. Can myself and Murdo, son of Angus, come a holiday to sunny Ealing? Ha!"

She backed the big Volvo onto the main road. She was a good driver. She drove off, back to the village.

With sitting in the trapped heat of the quarry all day, the interior of the hired car was like a furnace. I should have left the roof open and the windows down. It was a Renault Laguna. But who would steal a car around here? The two cars that had been in the quarry in the morning were gone. I opened all the doors of the Laguna to let it cool down and walked to the mouth of the quarry. The ben was purple in the evening light. I felt weary. The arguments with Willie and my sister had exhausted me. It was the same every time we met. They were cleverer than I was. My knee was hurting again. When I got back to London, I would need to go to my doctor for a check-up. Perhaps even book into a clinic for a week. Why not? I could afford it.

Back at the car, I closed the three passenger doors first, then got into the driving seat and closed the driver's door. The car was still hot. I pressed the button that let down the window and sat for a while looking out at the evening. The Atlantic was molten lead, calm and still; here and there giving off quick little gleams of silver. Behind the hills of Uig, the sun was going down in a sky red as blood, streaked with thin yellow bars of clouds; to the north and east, over our village and all the other villages in Ness, and the district cemetery above the sea, my brother's new home for all seasons, the long light changed as I watched, deepening slowly towards twilight, and night was a long way off. "I think I'll get a dog," he'd said to me on the phone a week ago. "Not a good idea," I'd replied. "Think of your furniture and carpets." "I'd keep him in the barn," he said. "Maybe I'll get a cat instead," he'd said then. He'd been drinking. Pressing on the button to close the window, I started up the car and drove out of the quarry.

But I hadn't driven more than a few yards beyond the first rise in the road, headed for Stornoway, when I found myself slowing down for some reason. What the reason was I didn't know. I only knew I wasn't ready to go back to Stornoway yet. So I drove the car off the road at the right-hand side, reversed onto a rough turf track, deeply marked by tractor double-wheels, coming out from between the peat banks, and brought the car to a halt with its nose pointed towards the moor. Switching off the engine and stretching my left leg out straight, into the front passenger seat space, I sat back. I sat forward again, took a plastic container of bottled water from the glove compartment and swallowed a lukewarm mouthful. Why, after three years of lean and sallow abstinence, of fruit juices, liver salts, fish oil capsules and expensive natural elixirs with all kinds of beneficial promises on their labels, did I not feel any better? Why was my mouth always dry, my hands still shaking? Why did I still have a pain in my liver? Wasn't the liver supposed to heal itself? I put the plastic container onto the front passenger seat and sat back again. A line from a Gaelic song began to beat in my head: *The sun going down on the west side of Lewis.* It was the second line of a verse in the song. I couldn't get the first line right, and I couldn't remember the third and fourth lines – *sight more beautiful than the sun going down on the west side of Lewis.* I couldn't get the first line. The moor was spread out all before me. In the late summer light, the heather glowed.

Almost directly across the road from where I had stopped was another track that went out into the moor. I couldn't see it from where I was but I knew it was there. Like the track on which I was parked, it started out between the peat banks, and where they ended, narrowed to a sheep track that led, by a route with many changes of direction, to a loch called Loch Leinebhat. It was the first track you took, turning off the main road, if you wanted to go on the Galson moor. It was the track my mother and my brother and I took, the day we went to look for the sheep.

When I was a kid, my mother always had a lot of sheep. I can't remember a time when we didn't have sheep circling the house going *baa*, dropping currants; motherless lambs, drowsy with Ostermilk and taking priority over the cats, in front of the Rayburn in cardboard boxes lined with old blankets. And when grand-uncle Norman, deciding that enough was enough, gave her all his own sheep, my mother was forever going out to an area of the Galson moor called Bhreisgro, where many of grand-uncle Norman's sheep grazed, to make sure that they were all right. Carrying a long, green canvas bag with hard, black handles, full of broken pieces of oatmeal and barley bread, pan loaf and plain, and a flask of milk for herself, she would set out for Bhreisgro in the early afternoon and return at nightfall, when worried small faces would be at the kitchen and bedroom windows, looking for her. Bhreisgro was miles out in the Galson moor – nearer Tolsta, on the other side of the island, than our own village – and my mother always went out there alone.

This Friday night, she returned from the moor at seven o'clock. From the window, we saw her stopping Henderson's car on the village road (Henderson was the local doctor; he called my mother Bo Peep) and some sort of altercation taking place between them, Henderson's sleek bull-seal head half out of the driver's window, his mouth rapidly chewing aniseed gum and his far-apart eyes narrowed attentively at my mother, who (arm upraised, index finger pointing heavenwards – *God is watching you! A judgement is coming on you!*) seemed to be doing most of the talking. "That's *him* told," we heard her saying to herself as she opened the scullery door. "Driving at that speed on the main road with no thought for the poor animals." Sitting on the stone step of the scullery in order to take off her sandshoes, she then started telling me (aged fourteen) and John (aged sixteen) about her day on the moor and how the sheep were. She had names for all of them. I wasn't interested in sheep. Neither was John. I was interested in football and Scottish dance music. John was interested in football, reading cowboy books and fishing. Padding on stockinged feet across the linoleum and flinging her sandshoes under the Rayburn, she asked my sister what was in the oven for her tea and could she have it in front of the fire, before easing herself, with a series of loud sighs, into the big armchair. "I'm nearly done," she said.

Later that night, after staring hard at me, she said, "Do you know this . . . on my way back from Loch Bhreithebhat, unless I'm greatly mistaken, I heard a sheep's bleat coming out of the bog at the head of the loch."

"What bog?"

"At the head of Loch na Saorach. Where they drained the loch long ago, looking for the body of a man that was drowned. There's a great bog there, sheep are forever straying into it. It looks so green and deceiving in places, and once in they get stuck and can't get out. Up from The Gil," she added.

"What's The Gil?"

"A stream in the moor. You've been there with me. You should know it. It runs under the ground where it isn't hidden by heather and comes out at the Galson river."

"What about it?"

"I just said. I just told you. On my way back from Loch Bhreithebhat tonight, I think I heard a sheep's bleat coming out of that bog at the head of it."

On Saturday night, she said to me, "I can't get that sheep out of my mind."

I had my ear against the wireless. Scottish Requests. Radio Luxembourg. Peter Jock MacMadron.

"Did you hear me?" she said. "Turn that noise down, Saturday night going into Sunday . . ."

Sunday night, she said, "Not one word of the sermon did I hear, for thinking about that poor sheep."

In my bed that night, I dreamt that a man with a black face was poking me on the shoulder with his finger. "You're for it now," he told me. "What have *I* done?" I asked him . . . and opened my eyes to find my mother, in a long white nightgown, hovering over me.

"Uh?"

"Heeesht!" she whispered. "Before you wake John."

"What is it?" I asked her. "What's wrong?"

"Keep your voice down. Remember that sheep I was telling you about? In the bog?"

"Jesus!"

"Stop that language! Remember that sheep I was worrying about?"

"What's the time?"

"Will you come with me to the moor tomorrow and help find her?"

"Three in the morning! It's three in the *morning*!"

"Will you come with me and help haul her out?"

I sat up.

"You heard, or think you heard, a sheep bleating . . . when was it? Last Friday? In a bog on the Galson moor."

"The bog at the head of . . ."

"Wait! Don't interrupt! Now . . . at three o'clock in the morning . . . Monday morning . . ."

She nodded happily.

"If she's been stuck in that bog since Friday," I took a deep breath, trying to be reasonable, "she's a goner. She's dead."

"No, she isn't."

"The ravens will have taken her eyes out by now. The buzzards will have picked her clean."

"No, they haven't," my mother said. "She's still alive."

"How do you know that?" I lay down again.

"I just know. Stop questioning me. Here's a cup of tea for you," she said then. "You're easier to deal with than the other one. Go to sleep."

When the door had closed behind her, I heard a match scraping against the wall on the other side of the room.

"John? Were you listening to all that?"

He didn't answer. I could see the red end of his cigarette in the dark, glowing brighter every time he took a draw, lighting up his face.

"What do you think?" I asked him. "Give us a drag."

"No," he said.

"Can I have the stump, then, once you're finished with it?"

"No." He blew out smoke. "I might go with you," he said.

"With *her*," I corrected him. "*I'm* not going."

"Good lochs out there . . . big trout in them."

"*You* go with her if you like. I'm staying at home."

"I'll take the big folding rod." He blew out smoke. "Want the rest of this fag? Here!"

The red cigarette end arced across the room and landed somewhere on the foot of my bed. I started flapping among the bedclothes with my hands in the dark, looking for it.

"Try the new fly Angus gave me, if the day's for it . . ."

"I can't find it," I told him. I flapped some more. "Jesus!" I shouted, beginning to panic, "I can smell burning . . ."

We had our dinner early. At one in the afternoon, we were in single file on the track of many turns leading out to Loch Leinebhat. John was in the lead, with a fishing bag slung across his shoulder and a folding rod in his hand; my mother next, headscarfed and sandshoed, cardiganed and overalled, grand-uncle Norman's stick in one hand and the green canvas bag with the hard black handles in the other; and me bringing up the rear, with the message bag I had helped to pack containing a large thermos flask of tea, a flask of milk, three mugs (including the one of King George VI and Queen Elizabeth), a blue paper poke of sugar, the teaspoon with the crest of Clan Maclean on it, a paper bag of cold mutton sandwiches, a paper bag of buttered floury scones (two with red jam), three chocolate biscuits from the Co-op and three oranges.

Above Loch Leinebhat, John made a short speech.

"I'm not waiting for the pair of you," he said. "You're too slow. I might try Loch Fhrasabhat on the way out. You can catch up with me there."

And away he went, along the gravel spit bordering the east side of the loch, and up the peat track that would take him over the mossy stretch of moor known as Blar na Fala (The Field of Blood), no one knew why.

"Why is it called Blar na Fala?"

"No one knows."

"Didn't grand-uncle Norman go swimming in this loch?"

"Not swimming, he couldn't. He used to walk about in her. That was his notion of taking a bath. He used to take a lump of yellow soap with him and a jute sack he kept for a towel. In the deepest part of her the water came up to the top of his moustache . . . Hello! The angler has arrived in Blar na Fala!'"

As she spoke, I saw a raucous squad of seagulls rising into the sky, circling and wheeling, taking turns to dive on something down below, and my brother John dodging along in the moor, waving the folding rod above his head like a sword to ward them off.

"Look at him!" my mother said. "That'll learn him!"

"We're not going the same way?" I asked.

"You're frightened, aren't you?" she accused me. "The seagulls won't touch you."

"I'm not going within a mile of them."

"You don't have to," she said. "We'll take a swing to avoid them, over to the hill of Loch Shiabhat, cross at the mouth of the loch and follow the old cutting from Chiapagro to Loch Fhrasabhat. There's Red John's hummock," she said, pointing to a nondescript lump of moorland with a hollow in it.

"Who was Red John?"

"A man," she said.

"And why was that hummock named after him?"

"He used to sit there all day."

"Doing what?"

"Nothing."

We walked on. She relented a bit.

"One of the Tams," she said. "Before I was born. He used to watch over the cows."

The ben, pale blue to our left, kept coming closer the further out we went – the Sharp Ridge, the Middle Ridge and the Buttock Ridge with the blue sky over them, turning white at the world's edge; the elongated "M" shape of Muirneag (the Maiden) in a faint blue mist further out, on the Tolsta moor. Climbing down into the old boundary cutting, we lost sight of the village houses, but not of the houses in Galson – for a long time yet we would be able to see them, looking back – the last three houses in North Galson – before the deepening moorland ahead took them from view. Broken banks of peat, topped with heather, formed both sides of the cutting, the bed of a dried-up stream, full of blue-veined, milky-white stones, went along the centre of it, and the fine black smoor under our feet made easy walking. My mother wouldn't go through the great spiders' webs, swaying in the sun, that went across the cutting in places. It wasn't that she was afraid of spiders. She wouldn't let me walk through them either.

"It's bad luck," she said.

The cutting widened at its end, opening out into the moor proper, and the long stretch of Loch Fhrasabhat was before us. We came out at the west end of the loch. Clumps of tall green reeds, almost waist-high, were growing on the near bank and out into the loch, and the bank itself was green and soft underfoot, like a lawn, with round, glossy patches of darker green dotted about in it; I knew the Gaelic name for them. On the far bank, John saw us coming and started to reel in his line. He didn't like anyone watching him fishing. He didn't disjoint the rod; he put the hook into the small eyehole at the tip. "So how many have you murdered?" my mother shouted at him. "It's too bright for the worm," he shouted back, as if he was talking to another fisherman. "If I'm not at Loch Sleat," he shouted, "I'll be at Loch Bhreithebhat." And off he went, the light-brown folding rod up against his ear like an aerial, the metal eyeholes glancing in the sun.

The moor between Loch Fhrasabhat and the foot of the ben is flat and soggy. Peaty, stagnant pools and small quagmires lie in wait for the unwary, between tussocks of wiry marshgrass, tangled and bleached by the weather. Walking over it in winter is heavy going, and even in summer it never really dries, and your foot can disappear without warning into a sudden bit of bog. We slogged across this stretch, not speaking; me in the lead. The ben was very close now, no longer blue, and seemed to be turning towards us, the closer we got to her.

"As if she was keeping an eye on us," I said to my mother.

"What?" she said, panting. "Keep to your right," she said. "Why are you going straight ahead?"

"You want to go in the lead? Go on, then."

"Shut up and keep walking."

Clear at last of the bad stretch, we started toiling through heather up the west side of the ben, beneath the Sharp Ridge. Clouds of small black flies, disturbed from the heather, formed

over our heads and accompanied us as we climbed. My mother
went into the lead again. There was no sign of John – then,
narrowing my eyes, I saw him, the wand of the fishing rod,
rather, flashing far below, in the glen of the Galson river. How
had he travelled so far, so fast? He was almost at Bhreisgro.

"He must have been running," I told my mother's back.

"Never mind him," she said, halting. "Starrabotter," she
said, pointing to the sunken course of a small stream emerging
from the back of the ben; a broad, stone-strewn vein of peat,
commencing almost at our feet and threading through the level
terrain below, met it on this side of the Galson river. "That's
our road down," she said.

"Why did we climb all the way up here just to go down
again?" I wanted to know.

"It's the road," she replied. "You're in the moor now,
remember?"

The Galson river. Dark pools asleep in the sun. You could
see down to the bottom of them through the tawny water.
At the head of each pool, green algae going over the stones
had hardened and turned black. My mother took off her
cardigan.

"The two Ealabhals," she said, pointing again. "At the side
of the ben, look. The Fair Hollow, between them . . . there's
a big stone up there, Dod's stone . . . that's old Dod, Donald
Dod's father . . . he was taking her home, for a lintel for the
barn, and he rolled her a good distance too before she got the
better of him and he abandoned her in the Fair Hollow. And
Bhreisgro, ahead of us, where my sheep are, look how green
and lovely it is, with the old sheilings on it."

"What's the stream coming into the river on the other side
of Bhreisgro?"

"That stream? That's the Gil. You should know that."

"We're nearly there, then?"

"You should know all these names."

"Why?"

She didn't answer.

"Now we'll see," I said, "whether this sheep is where you said, or not."

She didn't answer.

"She was there at three o'clock this morning . . ."

"We'll have to cross the river soon," she said. "I don't want the sheep on Bhreisgro to see us."

"You're not so sure now, are you?"

"In case they follow us up to Loch na Saorach." She swung the green canvas bag, nearly hitting me on the arm. "Stop your nagging," she said.

Like Loch Leinebhat at the start of our journey, Loch na Saorach is so low down in the moor, you can't see her until you are standing above her. But we could see Loch Bhreithebhat.

"Is that our John, on Loch Bhreithebhat?"

"Who else?"

"John Norman's loch, she was called, before they drained her."

"Loch *Bhreithebhat*?"

"Loch na Saorach!"

"Didn't you tell me she was called *The Catechist*'s loch as well?"

"John Norman *was* a catechist. He was drowned in the loch, and they drained it to try and recover the corpse. Afterwards, because of the effort involved, they called her Loch na Saorach."

A small cairn of stones stands at one end of Loch Bhreithebhat, near the broken walls of three old sheilings, overgrown with moss and fallen in on themselves – my mother knew the names of the families they belonged to, when they used to pasture the cattle out there in the old days. Small bright waves danced on the currents in the middle of the loch; further in towards the bank, where the water was thinner and my brother John was standing up to his knees, making passes with his fishing rod, it was pale blue and calm. I stood on a high, crumbly bank of peat and studied the flat, shallow water of Loch na Saorach, broken by small, half-submerged islands of reeds, and bordered on the side nearest to us by an unwholesome grey bog, extending in both directions and reaching almost to our feet. I had never seen this bog before. It looked much worse than the one we had crossed earlier. A steady hum of insects rose from it. There was another bog between Loch na Saorach and Loch Bhreithebhat. After setting the message bag down on the heather, shifting it by the handles till it was sitting evenly and wouldn't fall over, I straightened up and turned to my mother.

"Well?"

"What?"

"Where's this sheep, then?"

My mother shaded her eyes with her hand.

"Point her out to me, so I can go and fetch her."

"Be quiet, will you, two seconds . . ."

"Point her out to me with your finger."

"I'm still *looking* . . ."

"You're sure it's this bog and not the one between the lochs?"

"Yes."

"I can't see any sheep out there."

"How are you going to see a sheep without your glasses?" she said, rounding on me. "Put on your glasses. You'll have to go down into the bog," she said then. "You'll have to go out into the bog and take a look."

"Why?"

"The bog goes right in under the bank in places. You can't see from here. Maybe she's under the bank. Be careful," she added, as I started clambering down.

Down below, I skirted the edge of the bog, keeping in to the peat bank, until I found a raised tussock firm enough for me to stand on. Dragonflies, their wings a white blur, whirred against the face of the bank. I didn't like being near them, even though I knew they were harmless. Some of them were huge.

"Why are you skulking there?" my mother's voice asked from above. "Stop skulking there and go out into the bog."

The surface of the bog shimmered with an unhealthy,

greyish-yellow light. A stench of oozy, rotten mud rose from it; in the marshy places between the tussocks, saucers of flat, risen water, edged with petrol rainbows, bubbled and seethed; and lying in wait further out were the evil, bright-green stretches, grassy on top, that lured sheep into the bog to flounder and perish. I couldn't see my mother's sheep in any of them. I moved away from the bank, stepping carefully from tuft to tuft, testing each one with my foot before letting my weight on it. For all that, my feet sank at every step, the imprints of my sandshoes filling up at once with water, upon which, as I watched, tiny insects sped back and forth, making quick, criss-crossing lines. The bog hummed all round me with a life of its own. I didn't want to be out in it.

"Can you see her?" my mother shouted. I couldn't turn round. "Are your glasses on?" she shouted.

"Yes."

"Shout *kir kir kir*. Maybe she'll hear you."

"Shout *kir kir kir* yourself," I bawled over my shoulder. "I'm coming out."

"Look along the bank."

I turned round carefully. I had to keep shifting my feet from tuft to tuft. Whenever I stood still, I started to sink.

"Well?"

"Nothing!"

"Are you sure?"

"This is like standing on a mattress."

"Try to your left."

"There's nothing, I'm telling you."

"Take another look. Please! For once in your life . . ."

"No sheep here."

She was silent.

"Come out, then," she said.

"If there was a sheep out here," I shouted, as I slogged slowly back towards the bank on which my mother was standing with her lower lip out, "or an armadillo, or a unicorn, I would have seen her. This is like walking on a bolster. But there isn't." I scrambled up the bank and stood beside her, puffing. "What do you have to say now?"

"I heard a sheep out in that bog," she replied. "Not you, not anyone, will tell me different. Take that crabbed look off your face. Maybe," she mused, "she got out by herself, somehow or other?"

"Maybe she flew," I said.

"Maybe someone was out here last Saturday, heard her and pulled her out?"

"Why stop at one person?" I said. "Why not ten people? Why not the entire Borve tug-of-war team, with Big Campbell at their head?"

"I *did* hear a sheep out there."

"Here's John."

"Tell him to come for a cup of tea."

"Where are you going?"

"That hillock over there." She said the name of it. "Take the message bag."

She sat down on the heather and started emptying the message bag.

"John!" I shouted. "Come for your tea!"

"Why is he waving the fishing rod like that? What's the matter with him?"

"I don't know."

"Does he think he's still in Blar na Fala?"

"He's not coming yet." I interpreted the complicated semaphore of free arm and rod. "He's going to fish the other side of the loch, he's saying."

"You sit down, then."

"Might as well."

"And stop looking at me with that face. What cup do you want?"

"The one with the king and queen." I eyed the green canvas bag. "What's going to happen to all that bread?"

"Haven't I got sheep on Bhreisgro?"

"Ah!" I said. "Now I get it!"

"What? Hold out your cup."

"Now I get it! The sheep in the bog was only an excuse."

"What do you mean?"

"An excuse for coming out here again to see the woolly darlings on Bhreisgro."

"Liar!"

"The *pets.*"

"Liar, I said! What kind of piece do you want?"

"More fool me for believing a word of it."

I'm trying to remember what happened after we'd had our tea. I stood up . . . No. John was still on Loch Bhreithebhat. My mother said, "I'm not waiting for him any longer. Tell him we'll be at Bhreisgro."

Then I stood up.

"Take a floury scone over to him. And an orange."

I stood up. Sunlight on the water of Loch na Saorach dazzled against my sight, momentarily blanking out the bog in between. Or maybe I stood up too quickly. Through the darkened rainbow edges of my vision, a grey lump, like a stone, a boulder, took shape out in the bog; and as I stared at it, this lump seemed to move. A small vein started to throb in the side of my head. I took my glasses off, and put them back on again. The lump was still there.

I dropped to my knees and, using both hands, tore a large piece of dried peat from the crumbly face of the bank and broke it into three bits.

"What are you *doing*, boy?"

I scrambled down the bank without answering her and halted at the edge of the bog. The peat bank was behind me. I threw the first bit of peat in the direction of the lump and couldn't tell you to this day where it landed. I threw the second bit. Nowhere near. My heart was beating so quickly, I could scarcely draw breath. The last bit of peat I threw landed near the grey lump, to one side. And the grey lump turned its head.

"Hoi!" I shouted at my mother.

But she was already on her feet, her arms up in the air!

"Didn't I tell you! Oh, thank you God! Didn't I *tell* you she was there!"

"What now?" I shouted at her. "What'll I do?"

"We'll go and fetch her, fetch her out. Where's my stick?"

"You stay there. Are you *mad*? *I'll* go for her."

"Hurry up, then! Here!" She threw a chunk of bread at me, the heel of a pan loaf, it hit me on the chest. "Oh thank God, thank God!"

Out I went again into the bog, clutching the heel of bread in one hand, treading as lightly as I could over the tufts that kept sinking with me if I settled my weight on them, avoiding the soggy bits of bog between the tufts – the "living eyes" as they were called – to the surface of which sluggish bubbles of mud struggled and burst with a thick, burping sound. Moving like a high-wire walker, the stench of oozy, rotten mud in my nostrils, the steady, seething noise of feeding insects in my ears, I had almost reached the sheep when I became aware of a hurrying, splashing noise behind me. Before I could steady myself to turn around and confront this new phenomenon, my mother, with the green canvas bag in one hand and grand-uncle Norman's stick in the other, plunged through the bog past me.

". . . waiting all day for you to rescue the beast . . ."

"Are you trying to kill yourself?" I shouted after her. She wasn't listening. She'd reached the sheep – "Oh my darling, my darling!" – and was stuffing bread into its mouth, the sheep almost taking the hand off her in its haste to gobble it down.

"Look how she was trying to keep herself alive."

There was a black semi-circle of earth at the sheep's head, where she'd eaten the bog bare.

"What else are you but hungry, poor thing." My mother kept stuffing bread into the sheep's mouth. She was a small sheep with a brown and white face. "God alone knows how long you've been stuck out here."

"Why are you crying?" I asked her.

"Yes, I'm crying."

"You should see yourself."

"You're crying, too."

"No, I'm not."

"Eat, eat, poor thing."

"I'm laughing, not crying."

"Eat your fill. It was God and God alone that sent us here to fetch you."

I took my glasses off, gave them a wipe on my hankerchief and put them back on and blew my nose.

"Are we going to lift her out of it, then?"

"Wait till she eats this last bit."

I felt the sheep's ears for markings.

"Tip of the right ear, a rip below . . . notch in the left and a hole . . . Whose markings are these?"

"Alligan's," my mother answered at once.

"No stamp in the horn."

"That's Alligan for you."

"Come on, then. Take a hold of that horn."

"No, but you go to her hindquarters and start lifting and pushing."

"And where will *you* be?"

"Me? I'll be here, at her head! What a question!"

We stared at one another.

"I'm sorry," I said, "but you're making no sense. Now take hold of a horn, like I said, and I'll take hold of the other."

"You take hold of her hindquarters, like *I* told *you*."

". . . hold of one horn, a horn each . . ."

"Are you telling *me* how to haul a sheep out of a bog? Who was hauling sheep out of bogs before you were *born*?"

"I'm only saying . . ."

"What?"

"Take hold of a horn . . . a horn each . . . then the other hand under her front legs . . ."

"And *then* what?"

"Then – together – pull!"

"Go on, then. I've got a grip on my side. You wait, darling," she told the sheep. "We'll soon have you out."

"Have you got her?"

"Yes. What now?"

"Pull when I say."

"What now?"

"*Again! Pull!*"

"She's not shifting."

"You weren't pulling."

"Yes, I was!"

"You call that pulling?"

"You want me to hurt the sheep? Pull the horn off her head?"

"She's *stuck*! Haven't you noticed? Stuck *fast*!"

"You clear out of the way altogether."

"We've got to pull together, from *this* end."

"You haven't the strength of a *hen*."

"Both of you get out of the way!"

My brother John's voice, above my head. Where had *he* come from?

"Get out of it," I said. With his left arm, he pulled me away from the sheep. "You too," he told my mother. His shoes and stockings were off; his trousers rolled above his knees. His feet were black with mud; his legs spotted and splashed. Squatting like a weightlifter, he reached across the sheep's back and underneath her hindquarters with one hand, and cupped her under the jaw with the other. Slowly, his face concentrated and turning bright red with effort, he began to straighten up. He was very strong. He had medals from the big school in Stornoway for activities like putting the shot and throwing the cricket ball. With a sound like a gigantic belch, the sheep came out of the bog; a green stream that ran down John's trousers and legs squirting out of her as she came. A stinking exhalation rose from the green water beneath her, where she'd been fouling for goodness knows how many days.

"Over this way with her, a ghraidh," my mother babbled

excitedly. "Thank God you were here . . . to Alasdair Mor's sheiling." Her voice hardened. "Help your brother!" she ordered me. "You weakling!"

"I can manage," John told her. "So long as *you* keep out of the way. Take a hold of her back legs," he told me. "Wait till she stops crapping."

"Not long now, poor thing," my mother consoled the sheep.

"I've got her," I said. "What are you doing now?" I shouted at my mother. "Barging into people!"

"Stop trying to feed the sheep while we're on the move," John told her.

"Nearly knocked me flying!" I shouted.

"Wait till we're out of the bog," John told her. "Keep hold of her legs," he told me.

"Hold them properly," my mother said. "Don't hurt her."

"That's what I'm doing."

"Give her to me . . . you wretch . . ."

"Get away!"

"John! Tell him!"

"Shut up, the *pair* of you!"

In this manner, we arrived at the edge of the bog.

John set the sheep down. He stood holding her by a horn.

"She can't stand," I said.

"Go to the top of the bank," John told me. "I'll lift her up to you."

"Hurry up," my mother said.

John lifted the sheep up to me. The sheep gave a small groan. Up on the bank, she lay down and started nosing at the heather, trying to eat it.

"She still can't stand," I said.

"Never mind that." My mother's head appeared at the top of the bank. "Pull some heather till I clean her. Carry her over to Alasdair Mor's sheiling, a ghraidh," I heard her say to John; then, her voice breaking, "Look at her trying to eat the heather!"

"What's the crying for?" John's voice asked her.

"Yes. Yes, I'm crying."

"Stop it!" John's voice told her. "Or I'm off!"

"I will . . . I will . . . Hurry up with that heather!" she told me, in a hard voice.

"Here you are."

"Is that all you got? Get some more!" Then, rubbing at the sheep's belly and between her hind legs: "She has an udder, look. So where's her lamb? Her milk's still running as well, look. You keep giving her bits of bread, a ghraidh," she told John "No stamp in the horn, but Alligan's markings. So where in all the world is her lamb?"

I pulled handfuls of heather, John held the sheep for my mother and my mother cleaned her. When she had finished, we stood back and watched as the sheep got to her feet and trotted unsteadily to the end of Alasdair Mor's sheiling. There, she bent her head and started cropping the grass. Seeming to remember something, she suddenly stopped feeding, raised her head and gave a short bleat. And the next miracle happened . . .

Out of the low, broken moorland in the direction of Loch Sleat, a lamb's voice answered her.

The sheep turned in a half-circle and gave another short call. The lamb – we couldn't see him yet – was coming at a run, *maaing* all the way. When he appeared – a big, blackfaced male lamb – he nearly knocked her over in his rush to get under her. Her back legs lifted off the ground as he bumped and butted at her teats, suckling her, his tail going mad with joy. The sheep put her nose down to his backside now and again as if to say, *Hmm . . . yes . . . it's you, all right.*

My mother stood watching them. Her eyes were shiny.

"Where's your sandshoe?" I asked her.

"What? Stop bothering me."

"You've only one sandshoe."

"Who cares?"

"Look at that, John. She lost one of her sandshoes in the bog."

"Who cares?" my mother said. "The sheep's alive."

"You can't walk home like that," John told her.

"Who says I can't?"

"She can put mine on," I said. "It wouldn't be the first time."

"I was walking barefoot on the moor before you were born."

"Are you the same size?" John asked me.

"No," my mother said.

"Here you are," I said. "Put them on."

"They might fit," she said, pretending to study them, "if I take my stockings off."

"They fitted you last week, anyhow," I said.

"You're starting that again, are you? Turn your backs!"

"You spent a whole day in the peats wearing them."

"Still on about that, are you? Right, you can turn round again."

"Are we going, then?" John said.

We followed my mother along the small stream called the Gil – John was barefoot as well – down to the sheilings on Bhreisgro, beside the river, where her own sheep were. They raised their heads and their voices of different pitch and tone in a chorus of greeting when they saw who it was, and then came running. She fed them what was left of the bread in the green canvas bag, calling them by their names as she did so. They all had names. I offered the leader of the gang, a pushy sheep called Yellow Nancy, the remains of a scone from the message bag. She sniffed at it and refused it. "Go on," I urged her. "Gobble it up." She sniffed at it again.

"Leave her alone," John told me. "Can't you see she doesn't fancy the butter on it?"

"Good for you, Nancy," my mother said.

"Are you nearly done?" John asked her. "I don't want to go home in the dark."

"Barefoot on the moor!" my mother exclaimed. "How I envy you!"

It was late afternoon when we set off for home. The sun warm on the back of my neck, my feet padding on the cool, grassy banks and the gravely spits of the river; and every time we crossed the river, I could feel the slimy round stones at the heads of the pools, under water that wasn't cold at all. John led the way, carrying the folding rod in its canvas sheath. He hadn't caught one trout. Too bright for trout fishing, he said. When he said that, my mother turned round to me and pulled a face. She was happy. John walked at a normal pace. He wasn't trying to get away from us. We followed him, not speaking, putting the moor behind us. We were in no hurry. We were tired, like the day. Only once my mother broke the silence. "Yes," she said, in a strange, slow voice, caught up and carried away with her own thoughts. "That's the truth, yes . . ."

We came out of the moor at the Galson bridge. We'd followed the river all the way. John sat down with his back against one of the whitewashed cement pillars and put his sandshoes back on. A last long mile along the main road and we'd be home. It would be dusk by then. The end of our day. As it is dusk here, now, at the end of mine.

No moon tonight, no call for her. I sat on in the car, thinking. I didn't want to move. I took another drink of the lukewarm water. Three years ago, I went to bed one night, woke up the next morning to find that I had turned yellow. In the hospital, I was advised by a doctor that if a normal liver was the thickness of a fingernail, then my liver was the size of a finger. That was when I stopped drinking. I wasn't a drunkard, like Uncle Willie. But I drank all the time. I drank wine at lunchtime, whisky after the day's work, more wine at dinner, a liqueur or two afterwards and a large whisky, by way of a nightcap, before I went to bed. Civilised drinking. It nearly killed me. When they heard about it at home, Uncle Willie wrote me a long, funny letter – I have it still – and my sister offered to come down to London and keep house for me. I took another mouthful of the lukewarm water. A car bound for Stornoway slowed down when it saw me parked off the road, then speeded up again. One morning my Uncle Willie will wake up and find that he is dead. My sister, standing over him, wondering which pocket to pick first. Quite right, too. Keep it in the family. And blood is thicker than water. I don't hate anybody.

Dusk; and over the Butt of Lewis, one star opening its shutters. And no sound or motion tonight from the ocean which, as a child, on wild winter nights, would send me cowering fearfully under the blankets with its roar and reverberation. And out there on the moor, where I will never go again, Loch Bhreithebhat and Loch na Saorach and the roofless sheilings are quiet in the summer dim, under a moonless sky.

I wound down the window of the car. The sun had gone down on the west side of Lewis. How silent it was! How still!

I didn't want to move.

I keep busy in that great city where I have made another home and another world for myself, and where, amid the miracles of steel and glass and concrete, the never-ceasing tumult, the roar and reverberation of traffic, like the rending of calico by giants, the stir and bustle of the streets, the purposeful crowds, malodorous reek of subways, crash of cash registers, whine of lifts, insistence of telephones, murmurous tinkling of restaurants, days of no-sky and fine-grained, neon-suffused nights, I am far from the green place on the Galson moor called Bhreisgro, and from Loch Bhreithebhat and Loch na Saorach, and the small hillock with the name I can't remember on which my mother and I sat that summer's day long ago, drinking tea and arguing. But, sometimes, in my mind's eye, I find myself back there, and I see my mother, the headscarf pushed back from her head, black-haired, red-cheeked, beautiful, sitting across from me on the heather, and my brother John as he then was, up to his knees in Loch Bhreithebhat, working the folding rod back and forth with his young brown hand, the line looping in a widening circle above his head, before he sends it skimming in a long cast over the blue water. And at other times, when I am feeling low at the end of the day, the getting and spending done, and sadness comes over me, alone in my room, or in company in a restaurant, or walking the pavements of Ealing, they come unbidden into my mind, and I see them again.

I see them moving out of the glen, beside the river, the three of them; a lively, quick-moving lad in front, the folding rod on his shoulder turned to a wand of fire in the rays of the setting sun; and behind him, so far behind that I cannot hear properly what they are saying to one another, a woman and a boy, both carrying bags in their hands. But then, as I watch, other figures appear on the skyline, slowly at first, in ones and twos, moving down into the glen, and I recognise the terrible old men of my childhood, and old women in widows' weeds, and men who were never old, my father among them, entering my story at its close: and I think I know what is happening, as other figures come into view, streaming downhill on the Galson and Ness sides of the river, swelling to a crowd that grows and grows as more and more people arrive to join it, tall seafarers from the north are there, dark, driven Gaels from the south, and the dwarf people, my people, old as the ridges, come from underground to take their place in the tumultuous procession it has now become, marching towards me, but I also see familiar faces in the crowd, Mary Ann is there, waving her hand to me, and my Uncle Willie, book and bottle abandoned for the day, and my cousins Murdo and Angus, and Ishbel and Donald John, and my sister, aged ten, who knows how to keep house and light a tilley lamp and be brave and not cry if night has fallen and people still haven't come home. Out of the glen of the years I see them coming, the living and the dead come alive again, in the slanting rays of the sun that touches and blesses every place on earth, great and small, where people have lived and loved and died; and the men and women who were there once, in the houses gone back to ground, under the roofs long fallen in and vanished; and all that they said and did there, and all that happened to them; and the names they gave to those places where they wanted to be, no place too small that they didn't have a name for it, which year by year, like their language and their ways, fade from memory. In the setting sun, at the setting of my sun, I see them coming. And they are coming for the sheep that is lost.